Christmas Tales

THAT WARM THE HEART

VOLUME 2

SHARON CHARLES

Abundant Living Ministries.

Christmas Tales that Warm the Heart
Volume 2

© 2020 by Sharon Charles
All rights reserved

ISBN-10: 0-9759019-6-6
ISBN-13: 978-0-9759019-6-0

Abundant Living Ministries
541 W 28th Division Hwy
Lititz, PA 17543
AbundantLivingMinistries.org
email: info@AbundantLivingMinistries.org

Table of Contents

Dedication

To the memory of my dear parents
Frank and Mary Torry

who ignited in me an ardent love of letters,

who loved Jesus with all their hearts
and passed on His life-transforming story
to their children and grandchildren,

who provided Christmas memories
I will treasure all my days.

I look forward to celebrating
our Savior's birth with them once again
when my earthly story is complete
and we are all finally...
home!

Introduction

My favorite childhood memories involve stories.

One of my earliest recollections is squeezing next to my mother on an old creaky rocker while she read to me. I was determined to stay awake to the last page but often nodded off and she would have to carry her little girl to bed... only to repeat the routine the next night. There were many endings to great children's classics which I never did hear, but the memory of those times with my mother is no less sweet.

When I learned to read by myself, my father presented me with a copy of *Pollyanna* and invited me to read it aloud to him. I assumed his objective was to help me hone my newly-acquired skill. I realized later that wasn't his primary motive. He simply loved the message of that book. It wasn't long until I did too. He wisely knew the power of a story to teach valuable lessons and to make a lasting impact on the reader. To this day, I often recall that young preacher's daughter and her determination to find something to be glad about in any situation.

That was only the first of countless volumes that touched my heart. Night after night, I would lie with my head at the foot of my bed, so that I could catch a sliver

of hallway-light... just enough to illuminate a page. I was supposed to be sleeping, but the books captivated me. I would read into the wee hours of the morning.

Sunday afternoons, while my parents napped, we kids were expected to keep quiet and out of trouble. In our household, no sports, table games, schoolwork, or rowdy play were allowed on the Lord's Day. My solution was to develop a Sabbath routine... a several-hour retreat to my bedroom to savor a new book, along with the rare treat of a bowl of potato chips or a juicy navel orange. It kept my parents happy, while chapter after chapter carried me away to fascinating destinations.

Mysteries intrigued me, romances charmed me, accounts of faith, love and courage inspired me. On more than one occasion, God used a gripping plot or winsome character to grab hold of my heart and change me forever. I was particularly drawn to Christmas sagas. Many December evenings found me stretched out on the living room floor, devouring a new Yuletide yarn, beneath the twinkling lights of our Christmas tree.

Before I knew it, I was the one reading to my own children... and, in what seemed only a snap of the fingers, to 12 precious grandchildren. Along the way, I began dreaming up stories of my own, Christmas tales, a new one each year, until there were enough to fill a volume... two actually.

Introduction

You hold the second collection of these short stories. In the pages that follow, you will be introduced to an assortment of characters, some purely fictitious, others based on snippets of fact from my own Christmases past. You will meet Tatti, Aunt Allie, Friar Jon, AJ and others, from different times and different places. But the lessons each one learned about Jesus and His love are timeless and needed by all of us, young or old.

So...

whether you read (as I so often did) sprawled on a bed or living room floor, or settled comfortably in your favorite chair...

whether you nibble on a salty snack or sweet...

whether you zip through a book in one sitting, or savor the paragraphs over many days...

whether you curl up by yourself or gather with friends and family around the hearth...

I pray these tales will draw one and all to the Savior who came to earth that starry night over two thousand years ago. His story still transforms lives. I pray it has transformed yours. May you rediscover the wonder of that story through the pages of this book, and may the ageless message of Christmas warm your heart all over again!

*And she brought forth
her firstborn Son,
and wrapped Him in swaddling cloths,
and laid Him in a manger,
because there was no room
for them in the inn.*

Luke 2:7 (NKJV)

View From the Manger

I adored my father. He always let me shadow him while he gardened, or puttered around the house, or worked in his woodshop. He and Mom had named me Jennifer. But he called me "Kitten Little" and tickled me under my chin as though I really was a cat. It made me giggle every time he did it.

I used to brush my cheek against his gray-speckled beard when I kissed him goodnight and would exclaim, "Ouch, Daddy... your whiskers are so scratchy!" But I actually loved the sand-papery feel of his face, the ever-present smell of wood-shavings on his flannel shirt and the walnut-colored stains on his work-worn hands. I especially admired his massive boots, with the rock-hard toes and a random pattern of scuffs and gashes.

Besides Mom and my brothers and me, Dad had three other special loves in his life.

First was the Bible. He knew it from cover to cover. At least it seemed that way to me. He called it, "the Good Book," and quoted from it all the time... not in King James language, but in his own 8th-grade vernacular. "Man don't live jist by eat'n bread alone," he'd paraphrase, "but by all the good words God fires out o' His mouth." Then he'd add, "Ya ought t' eat a good helpin' o' them ev'ry day, Kitten Little."

His second love was woodworking. He created all kinds of masterpieces… cabinets, tables, and some absolutely amazing chairs… anything someone wanted, my Dad could make. It was his hobby but also his livelihood and he often said, "I thank Jesus all th' time that I kin earn nuff money to provide fer my loved uns doin' somethin' I jist love t' do."

And his third special love was dressing up as Rudolph the red-nosed reindeer… not just at Christmas, but many times throughout the year. He said he liked Rudolph because lots of folks are like that reindeer. They feel like they're different, not loved or accepted. But God made them all just the way He wanted. They're all special in some way or other. Actually Dad was perfectly equipped for the Rudolph role because he had a gigantic bulb-shaped nose that was bright red most of the time from being wiped with his over-sized handkerchief. (I was always glad I had inherited my mother's smaller smeller, and not his!) Throughout the year, at unpredictable times, he would don a pair of huge, stuffed-felt antlers and make us laugh with his boisterous rendition of the Christmas song.

Dad referred to himself as a redneck. As a child, I didn't understand what that meant, and wondered why he didn't call himself a "rednose." Regardless, I loved him and thought he was the very best father in the whole world... that is, until I became a teenager.

It sort of happened gradually. No lights flashed. No bells rang. But something changed in those early adolescent years. I just didn't look at Dad the same way. I couldn't understand the feelings I was having. My father began to irritate me. Things that had always endeared him to me now started getting under my skin. When my friends came around, I realized I was hoping he wouldn't make an appearance because I was certain he would embarrass me in some way. Honestly, didn't he realize my friends and I were too mature to find his Rudolph costume and dumb jokes amusing?

And his clothing... the dirty boots and faded flannel shirt... both of which I'd admired before... now disgusted me. Why couldn't he dress with more class, like my friend Amy's father? He wore a business suit and tie to work every day and, once when he picked her up after school, I noticed his shoes. They were shined to a brilliant gloss with cute little tassels on top. But Dad's boots were the footwear of a down-and-outer... clumsy-looking and just plain gross.

At age 13, I began to distance myself from my father. I'm sure he must have noticed, but it didn't change his behavior one bit. He continued calling me "Kitten Little" and doing the chin-tickle thing. By 14, I had come to absolutely hate this and would turn my head when I saw him coming my way. I no longer shadowed him and, by age 15, I dreamed up excuses to avoid him as much as possible. When he quoted Scripture in his uneducated vocabulary, I fumed inside. He seemed so childish. Even his craftsmanship that used to look beautiful to me, now appeared crude and amateurish.

About the time I turned 16, I concluded, "My father truly is a redneck!" (By then I was well-versed in redneck jokes.) "How humiliating!" If possible, I would have ignored his existence completely, except for one reason. I needed him in order to get a driver's license. I struggled to keep up a façade of niceness so he would help me get the required practice hours completed in preparation for my driver's test scheduled for the end of November.

Due in large part to his excellent teaching (although at the time I attributed it entirely to my own brains and skill), I passed the test on my first try. I was ecstatic, not just because I had a license, but because I saw this as a route to freedom. I could now escape from my embarrassing dad whenever I wanted.

The very next day after getting my license, I was exiting school along with all 600 other students, when I heard a strange sound. Looking in the direction of the noise, I was first stunned... then shocked... then mortified. My father's junky pickup was fast approaching. His head and shoulders leaned out the driver's window, with his reindeer antlers in full view and his nose looking redder than ever. He was waving wildly and hollering, "Hey, Kitten Little! Over here!" To make the situation even more unbearable, he had evidently bought one of those gadgets that makes a vehicle play tunes with its horn. To my horror, the tackiest version of Rudolph was being beeped out to the entire student body. Kids started to laugh and point... first at him, then at me. I wanted to disappear but there was nowhere to run and hide.

I walked, head down, to the pickup and climbed in.

"Hey, Kitten Little," Dad began, "jist wanted to cel'brate ya gettin' yer license. Thought I'd pick ya up and take ya out fer ice cream!"

The resentment that had been building over the past few years erupted. "Just take me home!" I snapped. "And don't you ever, ever do this to me again! I can't

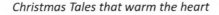

believe you'd embarrass me like this! Don't you ever even think?"

"Sorry, Kitt..." he started to reply. But I cut him off.

"Don't call me that! My name is Jennifer. I'm *not* your kitten. I'm *not* your little girl. Quit treating me like one!" He opened his mouth to respond but I ranted on. "Just take me home. *Now!* How could you think I'd want to be seen in public with you when you're in that stupid get-up? Why couldn't you, for once, act like other fathers?"

The rest of the ride was silent, but I was still seething when we reached our home. I stomped into the house and actually tried to slam the door in my dad's face. He caught it and closed it gently. I stormed into the living room and stopped in front of a strange-looking, long and skinny, obviously hand-crafted wooden object in the middle of the floor.

"What's that ugly thing?" I demanded.

"It's a manger," my father stated softly. "The church asked me to make one for the Christmas program."

"That's not a manger. It's more like... like a disgusting-looking dug-out canoe," I blurted.

"That's cuz I always figured a manger was more like a feedin' trough right on th' ground."

"Don't you even know what a manger looks like? This is way too low, way too long and way too skinny." Then I turned and sneered at him. "But, oh yeah... I forgot... you never made it past 8th grade!" And with that ultimate condescending blow, I exited the room, not looking back to see the wounds I had so savagely inflicted.

I wasn't proud of myself, but I wasn't sorry either. I was mad. I fumed in my upstairs bedroom. "Really... how could he act so stupid? Be so stupid? Why couldn't God have given me a more sophisticated dad?" My hateful thoughts churned on and on.

I felt like I just had to share my agitation with someone. "After all, misery does love company," I reasoned.

For a split second I heard my father's voice in my brain, "Throw yer cares on the Lord, cuz He cares fer ya." But I shoved that thought aside.

"Amy... I'll go see Amy. She's a good friend and will sympathize over all I'm suffering," I decided. With the impulsiveness of an angry teen, I slipped back downstairs, grabbed the car keys from the kitchen counter and ran out of the house. I would put my new-found freedom to immediate good use... or so I thought.

Halfway to Amy's house, it happened. To this day, I still don't know exactly how. I remember a truck horn

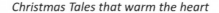

blasting and instinctively jerking the steering wheel to the right. Then, a tumbling blur of steep embankment, glass shattering in my face, and metal crushing in against me. With a chest-pounding jolt, I stopped moving. I was looking down, suspended by a painful strap. I tried to scream but nothing would come out. My eyes closed.

The next thing I knew there was a lot of noise and commotion... the sound of bending steel and the shrill whirring of a saw. Why was I hanging upside down? Why couldn't I move?

"We're cutting the roof now," I heard someone say through my mental fog. "We'll get you out."

For a split second I opened my eyes. A mangled mass of metal. Then... boots. Big boots. Familiar boots.

"Everything will be okay," I thought. Then my mind shut off.

I learned much later that things were touch and go for the next week. In and out of consciousness, I was reassured by flashes of my parents' faces. Once, I recall feeling my father's skin-cracked hand on my forehead and hearing him pray in his simple way, "Lord, Ya know we love our Jennifer. She's Yours, not ours, but we'd sure be grateful if Ya saw fit to let us have her awhile longer. Could Ya fix her up real good Jesus? Thank Ya. Thank Ya!"

God must have heard that prayer because gradually the fog cleared and, little by little, I began to feel twinges of strength returning to my body. Both of my legs were in casts and my head and chest were bandaged tightly. But I could at least move my arms and twist my neck and wiggle my toes. The day of the accident was still pretty fuzzy in my mind. But the doctors said I would be okay... it would just take time to heal.

And so, a couple weeks later, just in time for Christmas... December 24 to be exact...I was released from the hospital. Granted, with two casts, I wouldn't be walking any time soon but at least I would be home.

As the ambulance crew carried me through the front door, I glanced into the living room. The Christmas tree was up, decorated beautifully and surrounded by gifts. Beside it on the floor lay a strange-looking wooden object.

"What's tha...?" Like a sickening flood, the events that led up to the accident raced back through my mind. I recalled my anger and humiliation. How petty they seemed now in light of my father's tender care over the past weeks. I remembered the words, the horrible stabbing words I had spewed at him. "How could I have been so cruel to one so kind?" I thought.

"That's the manger, Jennifer." Dad answered quietly. "We used it at the Christmas program at church last night. Went pretty good actu'lly. Ya know... kids in bathrobes, foil haloes... like ev'ry other Christmas program. Ya didn't miss much."

"Oh yeah, I remember. I remember the manger," I murmured, embarrassed, now not by my father, but by the memory of my own sinfulness.

Alone and settled in my bed later that evening, I mentally reviewed the months that had preceded the accident. It's as though every single detail of that awful day strutted across the stage of my mind.

"Lord, please forgive me for all the hateful thoughts about Dad... and for the terrible things I said to him... and for the stupid way I acted. Thank you for sparing my life and thank You so much for blessing me with a wonderful father. A wonderful redneck father." I drifted off to sleep with a smile, picturing my dad with his antlers and red nose in his horn-tooting pickup.

First thing the next morning, it was Dad who came to my room.

"Merry Christmas Kitt..." he caught himself. "Merry Christmas Jennifer! Ya kin never 'magine how thankful t'the Lord I am t'have ya home!"

"Dad... Daddy, I'm so sorry. I was so wrong." The words tumbled out. "Those terrible things I said. Please forgive me. I wouldn't want any other father but you!" I was crying.

He bent over and wiped my eyes with his walnut-stained fingers.

"I forgave ya long ago." he said. Then he sat down on the side of my bed. "Ya know, fergiv'n is what Christmas is all about. We think it's 'bout a baby and shepherds and all. But that baby in the manger had t'grow up and die so's we all could have a clean slate. I of'en have wondered if, when baby Jesus was lyin' in that manger, if He wasn't already thinkin' 'bout all us people He'd be fergiv'n someday. I know I sure have had a crate-full of sins fer Him t'fergive. And He's always done it when I've asked. That's what the Good Book

says... when we confess our sins, sure as anythin' He'll fergive us and wipe all those wrongs from our record. When God fergives our sins, He never thinks 'bout them agin. Never, ever. And Jennifer, I'm not 'bout to think o' those things you said or did, either. Never, ever."

I blew my nose, now red from crying. "Thanks Dad." I reached up and touched his gray-speckled whiskers. "You know, I wouldn't really mind if you used my nickname sometimes... maybe just not in front of my friends."

"You got it... *Kitten Little!*" He scratched me under my chin. "Now let's go cel'brate Christmas!" He picked me up in his strong arms and I rested my head against his weathered flannel shirt, smelling the aroma of his woodshop. I would never be ashamed of my father again.

He carried me down the steps, into the living room, past my brothers and mother waiting patiently on the sofa, and over to a cushion-filled manger... just my size and ideally-positioned so I could reach the gifts under the tree.

"Dad, it's the best manger I've ever seen," I whispered as he gently lowered me into it. "This is the perfect Christmas!"

"Not quite!" he announced and disappeared into the kitchen.

In a moment he was back... brown antlered, red-nosed and booming out *Rudolph the Red-nosed Reindeer.*

He was right... *now* it was the perfect Christmas!

You did not choose me,
but I chose you and appointed you so
that you might go and bear fruit –
fruit that will last –
and so that whatever you ask in my
name the Father will give you.

John 15:16

Pick Me!

Will Jeffries packed the hunk of snow into a hard ball. Lifting his arm high, he took aim and let it fly. The head of Scotty Kendall's carefully-built snowman disintegrated! Will should have been elated when it hit its intended target but it just made him even more miserable.

It was Friday, December 15 and he was on his way home from school. Christmas was only ten days away, which would have made most 12-year-old boys happy. But it had been a bad day for Will. And the kid had experienced way too many bad days. All that he could remember of his short life had been lived in four different foster homes. Two of those had left him with an abundance of terrible memories. The other two were only slightly more tolerable. He was now in his fifth placement.

So far the Kendalls seemed pretty nice, unlike all his other substitute parents, but Will knew it would only be a matter of time until he would be removed from their home and sent who-knows-where. He longed for a *for-real, for-ever* family. It would even be fun to have an eight-year-old brother, like Scotty. But Will resented the younger boy. Scotty had everything Will wanted... great

parents, a nice house, lots of friends, even a decent amount of brains and talent. Will, on the other hand, was convinced he would never possess any of these. Today's episode at school had just sent him spiraling into a deeper pit of anger and sadness.

As he walked through the back door of his temporary home, Gracie, his foster mother, welcomed him with a smile.

"How was your day, Will?" she asked as she lifted a pan of freshly-baked Christmas cookies from the oven. But then, seeing the scowl on his face, continued, "Looks like maybe you had a tough one. Want to tell me about it?"

"No!" Will barked. Gracie handed him a cookie. He took a bite and then sighed… "I'm never picked. Never! Today, teams were picked for the holiday four-on-four basketball tournament. As usual, no one chose me. It's the story of my life. No one ever wants me." He turned to walk out of the room, then added, "Oh, and by the way, if Scotty wonders who knocked the head off his snowman… it was me." Will stomped out of the kitchen, down the hall, and slammed his bedroom door behind him.

"Lord help him," Gracie prayed under her breath, "and if You could give Jim and me some added wisdom, we surely could use it."

That evening Jim Kendall knocked on Will's bedroom door, pushed it slowly open and stuck his head
into his foster son's space. "Got a minute, Will?"

"Guess so," Will mumbled. He was lying on his bed,
hands behind his head, staring at the ceiling. Jim sat
down on the edge of the bed.

"Will, I won't pretend to understand all that you've
been through, or all that you're feeling. I don't understand why some people suffer many more disappointments and losses than others. Life can seem so unfair.
But I want you to know that Jesus cares about you and
what you've been through and so do we. And we all want
to help make tomorrow better for you, if you'll only let
us. Will, Gracie and I have a lot of hope for you. I wish I
could somehow give you a shot of that hope too."

Will kept staring at the ceiling. He wanted so badly
to sit up and hug Jim but he had long ago developed the
ability to steel himself against displays of affection. He
had to be strong. So he just kept staring.

"I hear ya," he said to Jim in a tone dripping with
sarcasm and cynicism. Jim patted him on the shoulder
and then playfully tousled his hair.

"Good. We can talk more any time you'd like. In the meantime, I encourage you to try to cheer up a little bit. It's Christmas, and no one should be angry or mad at Christmas!"

As Jim left the room, Will rose from his bed and went to the window. Looking outside, he saw that someone... probably Jim... had repaired the head of Scotty's snowman. Its silly crooked grin was even wider than before and his carrot nose bent at a crazy angle. Will cracked a hint of a smile. Perhaps he could dare to hope... just a little.

The next day, the Kendall family was buzzing with Christmas activity and Will had no choice but to participate. They headed out bright and early to buy their Christmas tree. Will had never experienced riding a tractor-drawn sleigh across snow-covered fields to choose a Christmas tree. There were plenty of bushy, perfectly shaped ones, but Scotty spied a skinny, odd-shaped White Pine and begged for that one.

Will was secretly pleased with Scotty's choice. Aloud, he just said, "Whatever... it'll do, I guess."

Pick Me!

Back at the house, they lugged several boxes from the attic. Working together, the Kendalls, with Will's reluctant help, assembled the stand, untangled multiple strings of lights and hung dozens of ornaments on the branches. By noon, the scrawny tree stood fully decorated in the corner of the family room and Will admitted inwardly that it looked really nice.

In the afternoon, Gracie insisted that Scotty and Will accompany her to the mall where they picked out some gifts for Jim. Will found himself feeling a little more upbeat as the afternoon wore on. The Christmas music, Gracie's animated conversation, even Scotty's silly gift ideas combined to lift Will's spirits.

"Maybe Jim was right," Will thought. "Maybe life could get better for me… maybe." He began humming along with the carol being broadcast throughout the store.

That evening the family headed to church for its annual Christmas banquet. Jim and Gracie assured him that he would have a great time but Will had his doubts. Upon their arrival, each family member was handed a piece of paper and told to print their name on it and drop it in a large basket by the entrance to the auditorium. They found their seats at a round table with another family from the church. Soon they were chowing down a really scrumptious roast beef dinner.

"So far, not so bad," Will thought.

The meal was followed by a Christian comedy group and even Will couldn't help but laugh at their performance.

The last item on the program was distribution of door prizes. The basket brimming with names of all the guests was carried to the front of the room. About a dozen beautifully-wrapped gifts were stacked on the platform and the pastor began pulling names out of the container.

"Pick me! Oh please, pick me!" Will pleaded silently. He had his eye on one thin rectangular gift, wrapped in silver paper. "That's the one I'll choose, when my name gets called," he decided.

One by one, names were called and gifts claimed. The silver package remained. Finally, it was the only one left.

Will continued his mental begging, "Pick me. Oh please pick me!"

The pastor reached into the basket, pulled out one more slip of paper and boomed, "And the last gift of the evening goes to... Scotty Kendall!"

Will's face hardened. "Figures," he muttered under his breath.

Jim reached over and put his arm around his shoulder, but Will scowled and pulled away. It was as though a coffin full of dead hopes and dreams had just been nailed shut and dropped into its grave.

Scotty returned to their table, his eyes shining and clutching the prize. "I'm not even going to open it until Christmas," he exclaimed. "That way I'll have an extra present to open Christmas morning!"

Will seethed. Once more he had been let down. "What's the use of hoping?" Will thought with disgust. "I couldn't care less about Christmas!"

Nothing Jim or Gracie said or did throughout the next week could pull Will Jeffries out of his bad mood. He sulked his way to and from school each day. He spoke only when he absolutely had to. He did his chores in stony silence. Even on Friday, when school let out for the holidays, Will remained grimly silent. All his classmates were laughing and talking excitedly about Christmas but Will watched it all with a hard heart.

At home he retreated to his bedroom whenever possible. Daily he found himself staring at the ceiling,

pondering the parade of disappointments in his 12 years. "It's not even that I needed to have that gift," he reasoned. "It's just that it was one more time I wasn't picked... and it's just not fair. Life's not fair. Jim says I should hope... hope for what? It doesn't do any good. Maybe for the Kendalls... but not for me!"

Jim and Gracie observed Will's increasing bitterness. They discussed and prayed and discussed and prayed some more. They were obviously trying hard to penetrate his concrete shell but nothing they tried worked.

When Christmas Eve finally arrived, the atmosphere in the house was strained. Only Scotty seemed blissfully unaware of the tension and kept a bit of Christmas excitement alive.

The Kendalls' church always had a Christmas Eve service, complete with a live nativity presented by children and youth from the congregation. Both Scotty and Will had been drafted to be two of a crowd of shepherds for the performance. Will had grudgingly agreed to this and had attended each practice with his kid brother in tow. Although outwardly he maintained an "I-don't-really-care-about-any-of-this" kind of attitude, inwardly he felt drawn to the story. It seemed easy for him to assume his assigned role. At the rehearsals, he secretly enjoyed imagining himself as a real shepherd living a rough and tough life in the hills of Judea. He felt a sort of thrill as the angels gave their amazing announcement and a genuine anticipation as he and the other shepherds made their pretend journey to the manger in Bethlehem.

Joseph and Mary were played by two senior-high students and the girl's six-month-old baby brother made a convincing, if somewhat large, baby Jesus. The child slept peacefully through every rehearsal and, since there were no other newborns in their congregation, this one did just fine. At each practice, when the shepherds bowed before the straw-filled cradle, Will would watch the sleeping child and felt somehow connected to him.

"Jesus had a pretty rotten start to His life, just like me," Will thought. Each time he knelt there, Will felt a lump in his throat and wasn't sure exactly why this made him feel like crying, in a good sort of way.

But all the thrills and enjoyment of the rehearsals were gone tonight. Will resigned himself to just playing the part. He would go through the motions, but his heart was cold and far from Bethlehem. Love... and family... and Jesus... and great joy... might be part of the Kendalls' lives but Will was certain those things would never be part of his.

He stood statue-like while the costume lady put a ragged robe around his shoulders. The make-up gal gelled his hair into greasy-looking long strands. She

rubbed dark smudges on his face to give him a grimy, unshaven look. Will caught a glimpse of himself in the full-length mirror propped against a Sunday School classroom door. He looked about as dirty and miserable as he felt. He lined up with Scotty and the rest of the grubby-looking shepherds and waited for their entrance into the candlelit sanctuary.

On cue, he trudged with the others up the steps of the platform and, like a robot, went through the "abiding-in-the-fields" scene. He faked surprise at the angel's "good tidings" announcement and then pretended eagerness to head to Bethlehem. As the narrator read the familiar Biblical account, the group of shepherds descended the steps of the platform, marched down the long church aisle to the rear of the auditorium, across the lobby and then back up the other aisle to the Bethlehem scene on the opposite side of the stage.

"And they came with haste and found Mary and Joseph and the babe, lying in a manger," the narrator continued.

Will and the other shepherds surrounded the baby's bed and, with bowed heads, knelt reverently before it. There was a holy hush throughout the room. The children's choir began singing softly, *Away in a Manger.* Joseph gazed kindly and fondly at his wife. Mary looked peaceful and radiant. It would have been a beautiful moment and a perfect crowning point for the presentation if it hadn't been for the shrill cry that suddenly erupted from the straw. Horrified, Mary reached down and grabbed her screaming baby brother who was definitely not performing *divinely* as he had at every practice. As she picked him up and tried desperately to jiggle him into calmness, he stiffened his body and pushed away from her. Twisting his little body like a corkscrew, he wildly surveyed the circle of shocked shepherds. Then, with one giant lunge, the wailing baby Jesus propelled himself away from his sister and toward his target... a kneeling 12-year-old... Will.

The surprised boy had no choice but to reach out and receive the baby from Mary's arms. Off balance from the child's weight, he felt himself about to fall forward but then, steadying himself on the side of the manger, Will managed to pull himself up from his knees to standing. He awkwardly cradled the rag-wrapped child against his own tattered robe and, although he had never held a baby before, he began gently swaying and patting the little one tenderly. As the choir finished the first verse, baby Jesus laid his head on Will's shoulder and stopped crying. A group sigh of relief swept through the audience.

When the children started the second verse, Will tried to hand the baby back to Mary but the child let out another howl and clung desperately to Will. Once again

he soothed him and, to the amazement of all, the baby closed his eyes and nestled against the young shepherd.

The choir finished their "no crying He makes" verse which brought ripples of chuckles throughout the congregation. But, as Will stood there in the spotlight with the now-quiet baby cuddled in his arms, the room hushed once again.

The voice of the narrator cut through the silence...

"Listen my dear brothers: Has not God chosen those who are poor in the eyes of the world to be rich in faith and to inherit the kingdom he promised those who love him (James 2:5)? God chose the lowly things of this world and the despised things... so that no one may boast (I Cor. 1:27). Jesus said, 'You did not choose me, but I chose you' (John 15:16). You are a chosen people, a royal priesthood, a holy nation, a people belonging to God that you may declare the praises of him who called you out of darkness into his wonderful light (I Peter 2:9)."

Will heard the words, and suddenly they made sense. He leaned his cheek against the top of the baby's head and smiled. "*Jesus* picked me. He picked *me*!" he thought contently. And, as the congregation rose for the benediction, Will thought, "Maybe I should keep on hoping."

On Christmas morning, the Kendalls and their foster son gathered around the spindly tree, gleaming with its tinsel and lights, to open gifts. When all the larger gifts had been opened, Will was surprised to see two small packages remaining. One was the "extra" present Scotty had won at the banquet. But beside it was another package... the same size and shape as Scotty's and wrapped identically. Gracie handed Scotty his gift but Jim handed the last present to Will.

The evening before had softened Will somewhat and he found himself feeling warmer towards Scotty. "You go ahead and open yours first," Will urged the eight-year-old.

Scotty tore off the silver paper and uncovered a small box of chocolates, which he immediately opened.

"I got so depressed over a measly box of chocolates," Will thought to himself. "Why, that wasn't a big deal after all."

Popping one of the candies into his mouth, Scotty said excitedly, "Now it's your turn, Will!"

The older boy got the impression that Scotty already knew what was inside his package.

"It's probably another box of chocolates," Will stated confidently.

Carefully, he peeled the tape and folded back the silver paper to reveal, not another box of candy, but a beautiful leather-bound Bible. Will's eyes widened and he ran his hand gently across the soft cover.

"Look inside. Quick!" Scotty was jumping up and down now.

Will opened the book and, on the inside flap was written, in his foster dad's bold hand-writing, *"Jesus said, 'You did not choose me, but I chose you.' John 15:16."* Will smiled as he recalled the words of the narrator. He chuckled as he pictured himself kneeling by the manger and baby Jesus flinging Himself passionately towards him... a dirty nobody of a shepherd. He didn't understand it all yet but somehow Will knew in his heart that Jesus was the key to never feeling unloved or unwanted again.

"Thanks. I really like this!" Will told Jim and Gracie.

"Turn the page. Turn the page!" Scotty ordered, still jumping up and down.

Puzzled at Scotty's enthusiasm, Will turned to the dedication page.

"Read it. Read it!" Scotty urged.

Will put his finger on the top line and began to read the inscription aloud, "Presented Christmas Day to **William Kendall** by his father, mother, and brother."

Will looked in confusion towards Jim and Gracie.

"We've completed all the adoption papers. They're ready to mail." Jim announced. "We'd love for you to be part of our family."

"For... forever?" Will stammered.

"YES!" Jim, Gracie and Scotty shouted in unison.

Jim placed his hand lovingly on Will's. "We pick you, Will... *forever...* if you'll have us."

With a lunge and a shriek, rivaled only by baby Jesus himself, Will threw his arms around both parents and then reached out an arm to yank his little brother into the joyous circle.

"And I pick you!" he cried. "I pick you too!"

*But thanks be to God,
who gives us the victory through
our Lord Jesus Christ.*

1 Corinthians 15:57 (NKJV)

Mr. G

It was an unusual mid-December cold snap that had Steve Clark's children pouncing on him with breathless excitement.

"Daddy, can we go skating? Please. P-U-L-L-E-Z-E!" his 10-year-old daughter, Mandy, pleaded.

"But Dad, we need skates!" 12-year-old Michael interjected. "Do you have any old skates in the attic? Does Mom? She said there might be a couple of old pairs in the attic. Would you look for them? *P-U-L-L-E-Z-E!*"

The children tugged impatiently at their father who, until a moment before, had been unhappily engaged in sorting through a stack of bills on his desk.

"Stop!" Steve halted them like a stern school-crossing guard. "I don't know why you suddenly have an interest in skating... but you can just forget about it. Admission to public rinks is expensive and you know money is tight right now. Plus, they are packed with people this time of year. And besides, you don't even know how to skate. You'd spend more time on your backsides than on your feet."

"No, Dad, we don't want you to take us to a rink. We have our own. Look here!"

Christmas Tales that warm the heart

Michael and Mandy yanked and pulled, dragging him to the dining room window. They pointed eagerly to the large empty lot adjoining their property.

"Well, look at that." Steve stared in amazement.

Just yesterday there had been an unsightly brown lake next door, due to the Noah-like deluge earlier that week, combined with mounds of bull-dozed dirt around the perimeter. But today, no doubt as a result of the sudden drastic plunge in temperature, the muddy pond had been transformed into a smooth sheet of ice.

Born and raised in Canada, skating had been an essential component of Steve's childhood winters. Like most Canucks, he had donned skates almost as soon as he could walk. By the time he was eight, he had joined a youth hockey league and his natural talent soon landed him a spot on the city's best team. He was fast and tough and smart and he had dreams of one day playing in the NHL. At least he had those dreams until he was 13 and then... he shook his head with disgust. Amazing that, after 21 years, the bitter memory could surface so quickly and with such fierce emotion. He felt his jaw tighten and he turned from the window, his thoughts stuck in 1989.

But Michael and Mandy persisted. They were not about to let their idea drop.

Steve willed himself to refocus. "Well, I guess they don't have to become hockey players," he reasoned. "I really shouldn't deny them the chance to have a little fun."

Like a jolt, long-forgotten emotion surprised him... the thrill and exhilaration of speeding across an icy surface on thin blades of steel.

"Okay kids...no promises, but we can at least take a look in the attic."

With exuberance, son and daughter clambered after their father up the steep stairway to the cavern at the top of the house. Steve reached above his head and groped the air until he located the chain for the lone light bulb. Soon all three were eagerly rotating boxes, searching for any labels that might suggest skates inside.

Mandy was the first to squeal, "I found some!"

Steve and Michael rushed from their hunt to examine her find and, sure enough, right in the top of a carton marked, "Save for Mandy," was a pair of girl's white figure skates. Mandy was down the stairs in a flash, calling for her mom to help her get bundled up for her first skating adventure.

"I sure hope you hung onto a pair for me!" Michael looked expectantly at his dad.

"Don't get your hopes up," Steve cautioned. "I think I told your mother long ago to get rid of my old skates."

The two continued searching and were about to give up when Michael, on his hands and knees, squeezed behind an old dresser in the farthest corner of the attic.

"Hey, there's one more box back here," he announced. He struggled to read the faded label. "Dad, this box says, 'Stuff from Mr. G.' Who's he?"

Steve's jaw tightened once again. "Let me see that!" he commanded gruffly. He pushed the dresser aside and slid the box to the center of the floor, directly under the light. He wasn't really sure he wanted to open it. But the call from his past was irresistible. Steve pulled the flaps upward and began lifting out items, one by one.

First a box of golf balls. Then a hockey puck. A Bible... it looked brand new. Next, several old CDs. Steve handed each item to his son, who had momentarily been sidetracked from his skate-quest by the discovery of new treasures.

"Cool... can I keep this stuff?" Michael opened the Bible. Inside the front cover was the inscription, *To Steve. From Mr. G. The words of this Book will change your life.*

"Dad, who is Mr. G?" he asked again.

Steve frowned, then shrugged impatiently. "His name was actually Mr. Grant. He was my next-door neighbor when I was growing up. He gave me lots of stuff. Probably everything in this box."

"Does he still live beside Grandpa and Grandma?"

"Nope... I heard he died."

Michael looked through the CDs. "I'd like to listen to these. The groups look kind of cool. I can download them onto my iPod. Look at this one... *Young Handel's Messiah*."

"Yeah well, it's not young anymore... that was an 80's version of Handel's classic."

Michael shrugged his shoulders. "I don't care. I want to listen to it. Can I have all these CDs, Dad?"

"Why not? Just don't play them loud and don't play them around me."

Steve was about to close the box when he realized there was another layer concealed by a piece of cardboard. Lifting the divider, Michael gave a whoop and pounced on the contents. There in the bottom were youth-sized hockey pads, gloves, a helmet, a Maple Leafs jersey and, under the jersey... hockey skates! Scuffed and worn, but they looked absolutely perfect to Michael.

"Whoo-eee! Were these yours, Dad? Do you think they'll fit me?"

"Well, they look a little big, but your feet are growing pretty fast. You can always wear extra-thick socks or stuff some paper in the toes. That's what I always did. Actually kept my feet warmer too."

Michael was reaching inside. "Yep, there's still paper in there. I'll cram in some more and I bet they'll fit just fine. Whoo-eee! Thank you Mr. G!" Michael fisted the air in celebration, but Steve barked at him.

"Don't thank him! You can wear the skates... but don't thank *him*."

Like a slapped puppy, Michael jerked from his dad's harshness. He made a hasty exit with the precious contents of the box. Steve tugged the chain to extinguish the light, his mood now as dark as the room.

Amy had married Steve, her childhood neighbor and playmate, just two months after they finished high school. The next four years were challenging as she worked to put her husband through college. After completing his studies, he landed a good job which allowed

Amy to quit her job and stay home to care for newborn baby Michael. Two years later, they moved from their tiny rented apartment to their current home, a small but charming Victorian in a quiet part of town. Amanda arrived that same year.

Amy never regretted marrying Steve. They had built a good life together. He was a hard worker, a faithful provider and could be lots of fun when he chose to be. She cared for him more deeply than when they first fell in love... but as the years passed, she grew increasingly exasperated with him. It seemed he harbored a smoldering resentment that could erupt into anger at the slightest provocation.

Steve had always dutifully accompanied her and the children to worship service and Sunday School each week. He even helped out with various church work projects and served on the finance committee. But he usually had a sarcastic, cynical comment after every sermon. As far as she knew, he never read the Bible and, apart from a memorized prayer they all recited together at mealtimes, she figured he never conversed with God at all.

When they dated, he had assured her that he was a Christian and he gave right answers to all her spiritual questions but now, 16 years later, she wondered if Steve truly knew the Lord.

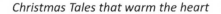

"We have super children, a nice home. Our relationship should be getting better," Amy thought sadly. But it was getting more strained every day. She reminded herself that her husband was under a lot of pressure. Wasn't everybody these days? There were lay-offs at work and talks of downsizing, possibly closing the business altogether. And now, Christmas was just two weeks away… that always brought extra expense. She was doing what she could to save money and tried to be pleasant and upbeat but Steve seemed more irritable than ever. Amy had faith that Jesus would take care of them and provide for their needs but, when she mentioned that to Steve, he sneered and rolled his eyes.

Although surprised, Amy was delighted to see his involvement with the children's new skating interest. From the day they found the skates in the attic, Michael and Mandy were outside every chance they got. The cold snap stretched on and the forecast predicted little rise in temperature until well into the new year. The children were actually getting pretty good at skating. Michael especially seemed to have a natural ability. Amy was glad to see Steve trudge next door almost every day to watch the kids skate. He carried the bench from their patio over to the lot and positioned it on one of the dirt piles so he could look down on them like a spectator in the stands. He dragged out the garden hose and flooded the rink late each evening, to produce a fresh smooth surface for the following day. And he rigged up a spotlight, so they could skate even after sundown. He did all that and seemed to enjoy it... but, when he came into the house each evening, he would sink back into his moodiness.

"Lord, I can't change my husband," she prayed every day, "but You can. Please... please reveal Yourself to him in a new way. Thank You Jesus."

Amy racked her brain to think what she could do to cheer Steve and soon hit on what she thought was a great idea. She would get him the perfect gift for Christmas. She searched e-Bay and online garage sales until she located just what she wanted... a pair of ladies' figure skates and a pair of men's hockey skates. They were in "like-new" condition.

When the skates arrived, she carefully hid both pairs. She couldn't wait until Christmas morning when he would open his present! Then she would produce her new skates as well, and the whole family could spend the rest of the day, skating together. Surely that would brighten his mood. She remembered how they used to skate together when they were kids... certainly this would make him recall happier days and cheer him up. Amy decided she could quit worrying about Steve and decided to focus on enjoying the remaining days of Christmas preparations.

Christmas Eve finally arrived and the family attended a late afternoon program at their church. Arriving back home, Michael and Mandy immediately begged to head over to the rink for a nighttime skate. Permission granted, they were out the door in a flash. Steve promised he would soon be out to watch them but he wanted to find a warmer pair of gloves first. Rummaging in the hall closet, he spotted a strange box under an old jacket in the back corner. Pulling it from its hiding place and lifting the lid, he discovered the two pairs of adult skates.

"What are these?" he demanded in the tone Amy dreaded. She kicked herself for leaving her gift-wrapping until Christmas Eve.

"I bought skates for you and me," she answered reluctantly. "I thought we could go skating with the kids tomorrow. It would be fun. The skates were supposed to be a perfect Christmas surprise!"

"Forget it! I gave up skating when I was 13. You go skating if you want, but don't expect me to join you." Then, through clenched teeth, he hissed, "You can thank Mr. G. for that!"

"What on earth did Mr. G. do to you?" Amy demanded. "He obviously did something pretty awful because any time his name gets mentioned, you get angry."

"He ruined my life. That's what he did. Okay... you satisfied?" Steve's voice was loud and bitter. Fuming, he slammed the lid back on the box.

Usually Amy retreated from such a display of temper, but not this time. Her heart was pounding but she plunged ahead with brave determination.

"Steve I don't know what you're talking about. I remember Mr. Grant as the kindest man in the neighborhood. Your parents told me he was a wonderful friend to your family. They told me how he stood outside in the freezing cold, night after night, to make a rink for you in your back yard. They said he went to all your hockey games and cheered for you. He was a caring Christian man. Why are you so bitter toward him?"

Red-faced, Steve exploded. "You want to know why I still get mad when I think about him? All right... I'll tell you! Mr. G. was always preaching Jesus to me... 'Jesus wants to help you. Jesus loves you. Jesus is always on your side.' I was foolish enough to believe him. I was getting really good at hockey. I mean *really* good. Our team had to win just one more game to move on to the championship. Winning that game would guarantee me a position on the provincial all-star team. Just before

that last game, Mr. G. handed me a note. It said, 'Just remember, Jesus wins!' It gave me confidence. I was so fired up. If Jesus was on my side, and Mr. G. said He was, I knew we'd win for sure! That man made me believe I was invincible... what a mean thing to do to a kid."

Steve paused then looked bitterly at Amy. "But we didn't win. We lost... lost in the last few minutes of the game. Don't you see? I lost my future, my dream, that day. I could have been a pro. I had to settle for second best. Yes, Mr. G. did some nice things but he messed with my life and I've never forgotten. He was wrong. Jesus doesn't help anyone win!" Steve snatched his coat from its hook and brushed past Amy to head outside but she grabbed his arm.

"I'm sorry you think of me and the kids as *second* best. My father always told me that life is way too short and way too precious than to ruin it by holding a grudge. Well, you've held a grudge for *decades*. Mr. G. didn't ruin your life. Neither did Jesus. You've done that all by yourself!"

Her husband shook himself free from her grasp and, without a backward glance, stomped out the door.

Under her breath, Amy added, "So much for my great Christmas-gift idea!"

Steve strode across the yard and plunked down dejectedly down on the bench. It was a crystal-clear starry night, a postcard Christmas Eve, but his eyes weren't looking at the heavens. He felt terrible for talking to Amy as he had but he just couldn't let go of that long-ago wound.

He looked across the ice at his children. They were having such a great time racing around the rink. It irritated him that everyone else could be so carefree when he was so miserable.

As Michael skated past him, Steve spotted a rectangular box on his belt and earbud in his ear. One more aggravation!

"Michael, come here," he demanded. "You know I told you not to bring your iPod out here. That's a sure way to break it. Give it to me... *now!*"

Michael sat down on the bench by his dad and dutifully unhooked the iPod, placing it in his father's open hand. Then he began untying his skates.

"What are you doing?" Steve growled. "Are you calling it quits already?"

"No, Dad. I plan to skate some more. It's just that I put an extra pair of heavy socks on tonight and the skates are feeling kind of tight. I guess my feet are really growing. I don't think I need this anymore." He reached into the toes and pulled out two crumpled balls of paper. He was about to toss them on the ground, but his dad stopped him.

"What do you think you're doing? Don't throw your trash around! Give them here. When you're done skating you can take care of putting these in the garbage where they belong."

Michael glided back onto the ice and Steve sat in the cold, holding the wadded-up papers and iPod and feeling sorry for himself. He glanced idly at the items in his hand.

"What kind of music does this kid of mine listen to, anyway?" he wondered and stuck the earpiece in his ear. A jazzed-up version of Handel's *Messiah* boomed into his ear. "Could be worse," Steve reasoned. And then it registered. This was one of the CDs they had found in the attic. "Will I never be rid of that man?" Steve thought disgustedly. Nevertheless, he found the music strangely soothing. He kept listening.

Absentmindedly, he began to unfurl one of the paper wads. "Interesting," he reflected, "I must have torn these from a newspaper 21 years ago." He chuckled at the 80's-style advertisements. Then, curious what other amusing ads he would find, he began to open up the other ball. Then he saw it... the plain piece of wrinkled white paper pressed among the newsprint. He began to unfold it but stopped short... a familiar distinguished handwriting with his own name printed boldly across the top. He knew immediately what he was holding. It was Mr. G.'s note given to him right before the fateful game. Frustrated, Steve was about to rip it up, but knew he couldn't resist reading it one more time. He held it towards the floodlight and read, "Dear Steve... Just remember, it doesn't really matter what happens in tonight's game because, in the end... Jesus wins!"

"In the end? In the end?" It dawned on Steve that he had never paid attention to that little phrase. "What did Mr. G. mean, *in the end* Jesus wins?" Gradually lyrics sung into his ear began to connect in his brain.

"For the Lord God omnipotent reigneth... Hallelujah! Hallelujah!" And then... "And He shall reign forever and ever!"

Like a heavy fog lifting, Steve's thinking, clouded for so long by ignorance and bitterness, began to clear. In his youthful immaturity, he had jumped to a wrong conclusion 21 years ago. Jesus didn't promise victory in a hockey game. And He didn't promise a disappointment-free life. He promised that in the end... *someday*... He would make everything right. That's what Mr. G. was trying to tell him.

Tears glistened in his eyes. He recalled Amy's pained words... "Too bad you had to settle for *second best* with me and the kids." His wife and children weren't second best. They were the greatest blessing he could ever have asked for. They were definitely a win. No hockey career would have been better than them!

Under his wool cap, The Young Messiah boomed. Steve reflected on Jesus' life. He had given up heaven for a dirty stable. He left His perfect Father to rub shoulders with a bunch of unreliable lowlifes. He surrendered His freedom to cruel Roman soldiers who beat and tortured Him. He was executed, though innocent of any crime. He lost it all... or so it appeared.

Steve had heard hundreds of sermons but, for the first time, God's game plan made sense. Jesus rose from the grave. He defeated death! He didn't lose. In the end, He gained a way to heaven for all mankind.

"King of kings and Lord of lords...Hallelujah, hallelujah, hallelujah!" The powerful refrain stirred his soul and he knew what he had to do. He slid reverently to his knees in the soft snow.

"Jesus, please forgive me. I've blamed You for so long, for something You didn't do. All the time You were on my side but I didn't see it. I really want to get back in the game... Your game, Lord!" He wiped the tears that were threatening to become icicles on his eyelashes and whispered, "And if You would… could You please tell Mr. G. I'm sorry too?"

Glancing out the kitchen window, Amy did a double-take. She stared in wonder at the sight of her husband on his knees in the starlight. She smiled. "Why, Christmas might just turn out to be merry after all!"

Michael skated over to his sister and, twirling her around, pointed to the silhouette of their dad, kneeling by the garden bench.

"Dad, did you lose something?" Michael called through the darkness.

With the last "Hal-le-lu-jah" reverberating in his ears and a new lightheartedness bubbling inside, Steve rose to his feet, waving Mr. G.'s note.

"No… no losses here… only *wins!*" His face beamed in the moonlight.

"Come on kids. Let's see if we can persuade your mother to join us for a new tradition… a Clark family Christmas Eve skate, followed by some delicious, steaming hot chocolate!" Under his breath he added, "And, thanks to Jesus and a very wise old friend, my wife and kids will get to watch me eat a hefty slice of *humble pie* besides!"

*...know the grace
of our Lord Jesus Christ,
that though he was rich,
yet for your sake he became poor,
so that you through his poverty might
become rich.*

2 Corinthians 8:9

Christmas
Family Secrets

C hristmas Eve. The tree in the corner of the family room was a beautiful, twinkling display of lights and ornaments collected over many years. Scent of pine boughs mingled with warm cocoa filled the room. A miniature nativity, comprised of mismatched figurines purchased at garage sales, sat on the coffee table. The tiny empty manger awaited the miraculous arrival of the Christ Child on Christmas morning.

The silver-haired grandfather settled himself into his favorite chair. Opposite, his daughter and son-in-law, cups of hot chocolate in hand, were snuggled at one end of the sofa. 14-year-old Alex, also sipping cocoa, anchored the other end. Sweet-natured and sweet-faced Caroline sat on the floor, leaning against the couch between her brother and parents. Now 12, she was looking more like a young woman than a little girl. And Jo-Jo, who, at age seven, had still not outgrown his baby name, climbed onto the arm of Grandpa's comfy "throne." He leaned close to his grandfather.

"Grandpa, we're ready for your story. What will it be about this year?"

Before he could answer, Caroline interjected.

"Grandpa tell us a story about you this year... something about the *good ol' days*, when you were a boy."

The elderly gentleman scratched his head and looked over at his daughter, raising an eyebrow in a silent question.

"Yes, Dad," she nodded. "I think you should share some of the family secrets with our children."

"Well okay," the grandpa's eyes took on a far-away look. "Perhaps now you're all old enough to get a little education about the Petersohns' past, although..." he paused, "the good ol' days weren't always so good. And the Christmases of my childhood weren't always very merry. But I do believe it would be fitting to tell you about the very memorable Christmas when I was 12. Yes, I do think it's time."

Five pairs of eyes and ears fixed on the old man, awaiting his story...

As you know, our family origin is German. I was born in 1933 in the city of Berlin. My mother (your great-grandmother) was a beautiful blond-haired, blue-eyed young lady... she actually looked much like you, Caroline. My father (your great-grandfather) was a young German naval doctor, tall and strong, kind-hearted and a deep thinker... a lot like you, Alex. I have many happy memories of growing up with my younger sister, Ingrid. We were normal children... just like you three. We got into our share of scrapes, and received plenty of lectures and discipline from our parents. We enjoyed playing ball and eating candy and dreaming of growing up. Those were the good days.

But then, when I was six, the war came. At first I was too young to know what that meant because my world was comprised mostly of just my parents, my sister and me. I realized years later how much our parents protected us from the disturbing events swirling around us. In spite of their efforts though, I remember them whispering in serious tones when they thought Ingrid and I were asleep. I can recall the troubled looks in their eyes, the worried glances exchanged and the absence of carefree laughter and smiles that had once been the norm in our home.

By 1944, when I was 11, I knew that terrible things had been happening in Germany and throughout Europe. I didn't want to believe the reports I heard about the prisoner-of-war camps, the horrendous cruelties being carried out in my own country. But I knew it had to be true because my father told me so. He had several man-to-man talks with me and warned me there was a strong possibility he would be sent on a mission from which he might not return. My father was a Christian and hated what the Nazis stood for. He told me he remained in the military because, as a doctor, he could care for the wounded and sick and share the love of Jesus with them.

"Jesus taught us to love our enemies," he said, "and that is what I will do."

In the summer of 1944, my papa put my mother and Ingrid and me on a ship bound for New York City. He felt the end of the war was coming and it would be unsafe for us to remain in Berlin. Plus, he had been commissioned to work in the infirmary on a large naval ship, so he would be away for many months and therefore unable to protect us.

My parents sold our home and most of our belongings in order to purchase the tickets for the voyage to North America. I will never forget clinging to my father before boarding the ship and begging him to let us stay in Germany. I promised him I could take care of my mother and Ingrid. But, with tears in his eyes and his voice trembling, he instructed me to care for them in New York. He told me he loved me and hugged me 'til I thought I couldn't breathe. Then he wrapped his arms around my mother and held her in the longest embrace I had ever witnessed. When he turned away from us, I heard a muffled sob coming from the bravest and strongest man I'd ever known.

Life on the lower east side of Manhattan wasn't easy. We had lived comfortably in our own lovely house in Berlin. Now we lived in a three-room, first-floor flat in a run-down tenement house. We had neighbors above us and on either side of thin walls. There was a vacant one-room apartment beneath us and my sister and I quickly took it over as our play area. Ingrid and I had no toys so we made some out of anything we could rescue from trashcans. I can tell you there were some pretty-strange-looking balls and dolls created, but they were all we had. We spent a lot of time on our own, because our mother was away working at a sewing factory. We all missed Papa terribly and looked forward to his frequent letters and to the day when we would be together once again.

We weren't the only German family in our predicament. A few others had also fled the war-torn homeland and, in New York, we soon formed our own little community. A half-dozen families started meeting together on Sundays and a neighbor of ours, an enthusiastic

young man, volunteered to give leadership to the little congregation. We were not looked on favorably by other New Yorkers. We were Germans... Nazis... enemies. We heard of many Germans who had immigrated to the United States, only to be imprisoned in their new country. We all lived in fear of that happening to us.

Our first Christmas in America was so different from the ones we had enjoyed in Germany... no visit from Father Christmas, no gifts, no big feast. It was really just like any ordinary day, except that my mother didn't have to go to work. I did like the decorated streets, the music playing in every shop, the Salvation Army bell ringer on the corner... but I would have enjoyed all of it so much more if my father had been there to share it with us.

In spite of our difficulties and pain, there were two events that helped brighten that first Christmas. The first was the arrival, two days before Christmas, of an envelope with the Salvation Army logo in the corner. The monetary gift inside, though not huge, lifted our spirits and allowed us to purchase a small treat for Christmas morning. The second highlight of that Christmas was attending church on Christmas Eve. Mama and Ingrid and I heard a hope-inspiring message about Jesus coming to this world, so that we could have life. I was convinced that, if God was as concerned about our lives as the preacher declared so confidently, He would certainly watch over my father and bring him safely back to our family. I comforted myself that Christmas, dreaming about what it would be like next year when my papa would certainly be with us once again.

My dream was short lived, however, because on January 30, 1945, the ship my father was on was torpedoed and all on board were lost. I remember my mother's shoulder-shaking sobs when our neighbor brought over the newspaper and pointed to the headline.

"How could a good God have let this happen?" The question hounded me. I had prayed for my father. I believed God would keep him safe. Bitterness and rage overwhelmed me and a heart-ripping sorrow like I had never experienced before engulfed me. Our family of three grieved... each of us in our own painful way. With no hope of seeing my father again, our household plunged into a joyless existence. We did what was needed to survive, wondering all the while where God had gone.

Then, Elias Bachman moved in downstairs.

After my father's death, the empty basement apartment that had been our playground became my "pit of despair." I would escape there often to brood, to yell at God, and to throw myself huge pity parties.

Then one afternoon when I descended the steps to the door of the apartment, I heard movement inside. I was about to retreat when a booming bass voice called,

"Come in! Door's open!"

Cautiously I pushed open the door. A giant of a man stood in the middle of the room. He wasn't old... definitely not young though. I decided he was what my mother called "jung -mitte" or young middle-aged. Black wavy hair, dark penetrating eyes, a crooked nose and an unsightly scar running from his hairline to his chin. He had a wide smile that kept me from high-tailing it out of there.

"Come in. Come in, my friend!" With great drama, he motioned me to the solitary chair in the middle of the room. "My first visitor!" he exclaimed in an accent that was definitely German but with a twist I couldn't quite identify. Our new neighbor gestured toward the ceiling.

"What a blessing from the Lord! Kommen sie und sit awhile. Allow me to introduce myself. I am Elias Bachman and you are...?" As he reached out his left hand to shake mine, I saw that his right hand hung limply at his side.

"I'm Alexander Petersohn," I replied as I moved to the chair and sat, as ordered. I did a quick survey of the apartment. The concrete floor that had always been littered with trash and leaves was now swept clean. The once-bare room held a small table and a single chair on which I was sitting. On the table was a lone book... a Bible perhaps? Against the wall there were a couple of rickety crates turned on end. On top of one was a two-burner hotplate and stacked inside were a pot and lid, a couple of plates and utensils, a few cans of baked beans, and a jar of peanut butter. The other wooden box contained a few articles of clothing. In the corner of the room a thin blanket was spread on the floor, with another blanket neatly folded and placed at one end of it. And at the other end, a small gray metal box.

"Not a very comfortable pillow," I thought, as I viewed the make-shift bed. On the wall opposite the bed an almost-sheer curtain hung across the entrance to the tiny bathroom, which I already knew contained only a commode and pitifully-small washbowl. But I could tell both had been cleaned and looked far more sanitary than when I played there.

"So young man... my new American friend... tell me all about yourself. Where do you live? Upstairs? Ah, how wonderful. We're friends and neighbors too!"

"You don't have very much furniture... or anything else for that matter," I blurted.

"Ja, my friend... you are right. But that's okay... I started out with nothing and I still have most of it!" He threw his head back and laughed at his own joke.

I had no idea at that moment just how special Mr. Bachman would become to me and my family. Over the next weeks and months, he became my best friend. I could tell him anything... even how angry I was with God for allowing my father to die. He listened compassionately, like he understood my pain. He could even make me laugh sometimes... and it felt good to laugh again. But, in spite of our many great chats, Mr. Bachman couldn't free me of the bitterness that was strangling my heart.

Mr. Bachman began attending our little church. He always sat alone in the back row and I wondered why no one talked much with him. When we rose to sing our hymns, I could count on hearing his bass voice above the rest of the congregation. He sang beautifully. And when our pastor read from the Bible, it was Mr. Bachman's "amens" that seemed to make the words more believable. Still, no one chatted with him, except for me. I asked my mother why folks weren't friendly towards him.

"I think it's because he's a little different... and sometimes that scares people. But I'm sure he must be nice, because you say that he is. Perhaps someday we could have him over."

I knew that was not about to happen though. My mother had no time, strength, or money for entertaining. It was all she could do to keep us from becoming homeless. I watched her becoming more and more tired and discouraged and it only made me angrier.

As the year progressed, not only did my anger grow, but so did fear. Without my father's regular paychecks, our financial situation became desperate. Mama worked longer hours at the factory but still, each month, we were slipping further into debt. Not able to correspond with her husband anymore, she began to unload her misery on me and I was constantly reminded of the promise I had made to my dad to care for Mother and Ingrid in New York City. But I was only 12 and it was 1945 and there was little work for adults, never mind youngsters.

The weeks and months marched by and, when December of 1945 rolled around, our family was on the verge of becoming destitute. And we definitely weren't the only ones suffering. Every family in our church was struggling to keep a roof over their heads and food on their tables.

I hated all the sights and sounds of Christmas that year. What was there to be joyful about? At least the year before, I had the hope of being reunited with my father. That helped make our poverty more bearable. But this year, hope was gone and only anger remained.

I should have felt some optimism because the war was finally over but we were still looked upon by many New Yorkers as "those evil Nazi Germans." My family hadn't committed the atrocities. We hadn't killed all those innocent people. Why should we be blamed for something we had no part in? Life seemed so unfair. My anger kept growing.

When Christmas week arrived, I resolved I had to do something to help us get money. I went house-to-house on the lower east side, offering to do any odd job. But many didn't want to employ a Deutschlander... and many were as poor as we were. On December 23, in desperation, I swallowed my pride and spoke to one of the Salvation Army bell ringers, pleading with him to help not only my family but also the rest in our little church. At first, the man seemed genuinely concerned. He even had me write down the names of each of the families in our congregation. He assured me he would see what he could do. Then he read down my list and I saw his expression change.

"But you must remember there are many other immigrants that need help," he said. I knew what he meant... others that were more important than Germans. I left him, feeling humiliated and hopeless. In his eyes, I was just a hated Nazi kid... an enemy. He wouldn't care about us. And he certainly wouldn't fix our problems.

In my mind there was only one option left. I would have to resort to *stealing*... some food, some money... anything to help us. I had always been taught that stealing was a sin. But I didn't believe in obeying God's rules anymore. Where had that gotten my father? Where had it gotten my family? I began formulating the plans for my first crime.

It was my habit to stop in every day to see Mr. Bachman and, as I look back now, I realize that the talks we had that year had undoubtedly kept me from doing some pretty stupid things. I might have resorted to theft much sooner if it hadn't been for his calm encouragement. I didn't understand how he could be so cheerful when he was just as impoverished as my family... maybe more so. At least we had beds and pillows. He only had the hard floor to sleep on with a metal box beneath his head. How could he live like that and maintain such a joyful attitude?

I think the encounter with the bell ringer was too much for me. As I descended the steps to Mr. Bachman's apartment that afternoon, my temper was about to explode. I pushed open his always-unlocked door and found him dancing around the room with an invisible dance partner, singing *O Tannenbaum.*

"Come in my friend," he bellowed. "Sing with me. Let's be merry! It's almost Christmas. Let's have a party for our Messiah!"

Usually his cheerfulness comforted me, but that day it infuriated me.

"How can you even talk about being merry?" I erupted. "You have nothing. No decent food. No money. You sleep on the *floor!* No one even likes you!" Now I was in a rage and all the pent-up emotion I'd been carrying for months came spewing out. I pointed to his scarred face and useless arm.

"And you're an ugly cripple besides!" Hot tears blurred my vision, but didn't blind my eyes to the wounded look on my friend's face.

I turned and raced up the stairs to our apartment. I flung myself on my bed and pummeled my pillow, all the while screaming at God for every miserable hurt of my life. I cried and cried and finally cried myself to sleep... but not before I had come to two important conclusions...

"Tomorrow, I will become a thief and I will be a good one!" I decided. "And, I am done with Mr. Bachman and his pie-in-the-sky attitude and Jesus talk." Life had been nothing but hard for me, so I would become hard myself. I would survive, and I would do it my way, not God's way... and definitely not Mr. Bachman's. I resolved that the next day would be the start of a new life for young Alexander Petersohn.

As I lay in bed the next morning, I actually enjoyed plotting my first theft. It was Christmas Eve and stores would be open late and filled with last-minute shoppers. There was a jewelry store a few blocks away. How difficult could it be to slip a ring or bracelet into my pocket when the clerk wasn't looking? I formulated all the details of the heist and I was convinced that I could pull it off successfully. I found I was filled with a strange nervous anticipation, but I knew I must not let my mother or Ingrid suspect that anything was out of the ordinary.

So, the rest of the day I avoided them as much as possible until late afternoon when my mother announced it was time to head to church for the Christmas Eve service. I hated the thought of hearing another sermon from that annoying and now-judged-by-me-to-be-stupid pastor but at least it would keep my mother and sister from watching me too closely. I could easily slip away from them after the service, with the excuse that I wanted to enjoy a walk in the snow that had begun to fall. If I would have been on speaking terms with God, I would have thanked Him for that snow which provided a great reason for me to get away on my own.

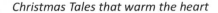
The church was filled with the same few faithful families that always attended. I looked around. What a sorry lot they were... all refugees in a foreign land... paupers pretending to have hope when I knew they had none.

"This church is pitiful," I thought. Two ridiculously-small poinsettias sat forlornly on the communion table and odds and ends of old candles provided dim light. A dozen little children in ragged clothes sang *Away in a Manger* and, as I bitterly analyzed the song, I concluded it was a lie.

... *no crying He makes...* "If Jesus had truly been without a bed, he would have made lots of crying," I reasoned. "And if He was really God, why would He choose to live like a down-and-outer?" It made no sense.

I tuned out the pastor's sermon and was glad when we stood to sing the last carol. My mouth formed the words but inside I was rehearsing the events soon to follow. It infuriated me to hear Mr. Bachman's voice, joyful and triumphant, from the back corner.

"Such a foolish man," I thought and chose to ignore the ache I felt in my heart when I thought about my decision to sever our friendship.

The pastor stepped out from behind the pulpit and opened his Bible. I waited for him to pronounce the benediction but instead he held up several white envelopes.

"Friends," he smiled hugely. "I know this has been a hard year for us. And we have been praying and trusting the Lord to get us through. Well, this Christmas Eve, I believe that He has answered our prayers! This very afternoon a package was delivered to me. It contained these envelopes... one for each family in our congregation. When I call your name, you may come and receive your gift."

As the representatives from each family returned to their seats and opened their envelopes, I began to hear gasps followed by cries of joy and even saw men breaking into tears. So when my mother approached our row, Ingrid and I leaned in eagerly as she lifted the paper flap. What we saw brought our own gasps! I thought for a moment that my mother would faint. Inside was not just a single one-hundred-dollar bill but ten one-hundred-dollar bills. A thousand dollars! I knew that was more than my mother would make in a whole year! We couldn't believe it. For a split second, I thought that perhaps there might be a God after all. Or maybe my plea to the Salvation Army had worked a miracle.

"*Of course...* it had to be that!" I concluded. I had given the bell ringer all the names. Was it possible his agency chose our tiny community as their special

project? I turned to look for my friend. He wasn't there. Suddenly I realized that Mr. Bachman's name had not been called and, even worse, with a sickening feeling in the pit of my stomach, I realized I had failed to include his name on the list I gave to the bell ringer.

"Mother," I felt a desperate urgency, "I don't think Mr. Bachman received an envelope. We have to do something for him."

"Ja, of course, we will!" Mother was laughing and it was the first laughter I had heard since my father had died. "We will have him for dinner tomorrow."

"And may I buy him a gift?" I pleaded.

"Ja, ja… of course! Nothing extravagant, because we must budget this carefully in order to get back on our feet, but God has been so generous and kind. How can we not be as well?" She laughed again and pulled Ingrid and me into her arms.

In just a few short moments, my Christmas Eve plot had been turned thoroughly upside down. Instead of heading out alone into the snow to rob a jewelry store, I was heading out with my mother and sister to buy food for a thanksgiving-filled Christmas, as well as a gift for my friend … and I knew exactly what I would buy.

On the way home from our shopping excursion that Christmas Eve, I stopped in at Mr. Bachman's. I needed to invite him to join us the next day as well as apologize for all the hateful things I had said to him the day before.

"No need to worry, my friend," he boomed. "You were forgiven before you even stepped out of my house yesterday. You have carried quite a load this year, but something seems to have lifted some of your gloom. I don't know what, but I'm glad for you. Now run along and get some sleep... I'll see you tomorrow to celebrate Jesus' birthday!"

Our Christmas dinner with Mr. Bachman was filled with true Yuletide cheer. I still missed my father terribly, but our Christmas Eve miracle had made me dare to hope for better days ahead. When the meal was over, Mr. Bachman offered to help my mother wash the dishes and I heard them chatting pleasantly as they cleared the table together. They were obviously enjoying themselves. That provided the perfect opportunity for me to slip downstairs with the gift we had purchased the evening before. Under the pretext of taking out a bag of trash, I hurried to my friend's simple home. As I pushed open the door, I pulled a plump, feather pillow from the

decoy bag. My mother had tied a red ribbon around it and I couldn't wait to replace his steel box with this soft improvement.

As I bent and grabbed the box to slide it out of the way, its lid lifted. I was startled that it opened so easily and my curiosity was aroused... what did Mr. Bachman keep in this old metal container anyway? I set the pillow down, and knelt on the floor, quietly and cautiously raising the lid of my neighbor's box.

The inside was stuffed full of small velvet pouches. Without counting them all, I guessed there were at least twenty tiny bags. Curiosity mounting, I carefully opened one. I was no gem expert, but the contents sure looked like diamonds... big ones! My thoughts raced. Was Mr. Bachman a thief? If he had all these jewels, why would he live like a tramp? Then I spied a yellowed newspaper clipping stuck against the underside of the lid. Gingerly, I unfolded it. There was a photograph of a family... a gray-haired couple and a young couple. The young husband cradled an infant in his arms and his wife held the hand of a dark-haired, beautiful little girl. They were standing in front of an enormous house... it looked like a palace to me. The German headline read, "Diamond-trading Family Purchases Estate Near Munich." I began reading: "Wealthy jewelers, Elias Bachman Sr. and Elias Bachman, Jr. will soon move with their families into their newly-acquired regal homestead." I quit reading

and looked at the photo once again. Of course... the tall young man in the picture had to be my friend, Elias Bachman, Jr. He was minus the scar and he was cuddling his baby in what appeared to be a perfectly-normal, strong right arm. I studied each of the people carefully.

"Hold on," I thought to myself. "They're *Jews*. Mr. Bachman is *Jewish!*" I muttered.

"So you've discovered my secret, have you, my friend?" the familiar bass voice almost scared me out of my boots.

"I'm so sorry, Mr. Bachman. I was wrong to look in the box." Two apologies in two days... definitely a record for me.

"Shush, shush, my Alex. I do not mind. Curiosity may have killed the cat, but it won't kill you, at least not this time," he chuckled.

"But I don't understand," I exclaimed.

"Let me help you, then." He pulled his chair over close and sat down.

"Yes, Alexander, I am a German Jew. My family bought and sold diamonds and made a lot of money doing it. We loved each other and had a very comfortable life. Then the war began and the Nazis came and my family was torn apart." He paused and squeezed his eyes shut for a moment, as though remembering, but not wanting to.

"We were separated and sent to different prison camps. I witnessed unspeakable cruelty in my camp. I shudder when I think what my family must have also gone through. And I was powerless to help them. I was furious with myself, with God, and with every German. Sometimes I wanted to die but mostly I wanted to live so I could somehow get revenge on my enemies.

"I was put to work repairing train tracks. We labored each day from dawn until dark, way past the point of exhaustion. One day, a prisoner who was working near me collapsed and I left my spot to go and assist him. The guard came charging at me with his rifle. He shoved the butt end of the gun into my stomach. Oy... it hurt like nothing I had ever experienced! I doubled over and when I looked up the rifle was descending on me again, this time right towards my face. I reached up to shield myself from its blows but it was no use. Then all went black.

"When I regained consciousness, I was in a soft bed. I learned later that my rescuer was a poor farmer who had come upon me lying in the ditch by the side of the railroad track. Evidently, the guard assumed I was dead and simply abandoned me there. My deliverer and his sweet wife took care of my wounds as best they could and kept me safe and hidden. You know the story of the good Samaritan in the Bible? Well, Herr Althaus was my good Samaritan... and not just because he nursed me back to health... but because he shared with me the story of Jesus.

"At first I was so, so bitter and I would unleash my rage in torrents of horrible words. But my friend always forgave, and kept on loving and telling me about Jesus. It took months but finally, one day, I realized what he was saying had to be true. The Nazi's hate was strong but I had come to see that this Christian man's love was much stronger. I quit doubting and put trust in my Messiah."

"But how did you get all these diamonds? And how did you end up here? And why..." I had so many questions, I couldn't get them out fast enough.

"Ah, you're getting ahead of me, mein freund. When I regained strength, I went back to our house... the one you see in the picture. I travelled disguised. There were several close calls, when I was almost recaptured, but the Lord protected me. Our lovely home was in shambles. Nazis had stripped it of its priceless contents and damaged it beyond repair. But I knew where my father had hidden a huge stash of diamonds. He had wisely sensed the approaching danger of the war and he wanted to provide for us. I found the diamonds behind a loose brick in one of the outbuildings and I squeezed each one into the hems of my clothing." He chuckled.

"It weighed me down considerably, but no one guessed the fortune that was concealed on me. The diamonds allowed me to pay for information, but the result was not what I wanted to hear. I learned which camps my family had been sent to and learned that not one of my precious loved ones had survived. My darling wife, my parents..." his voice broke, "and my children... my dear, dear little ones... all gone from me forever! It saddened me beyond words... and still does," he paused. "But it did not shake my newfound faith. I knew Jesus had saved me and somehow, in my heart, I was assured that my family members had found Jesus too. I am at peace that they are safe with Him.

"I had no reason to stay in Europe, so I decided I would get a fresh start in America. I purposed that, just as my farmer friend had rescued me... me, a *Jew*... someone he was supposed to hate and annihilate... and just as Jesus had left his grand home in heaven to come and rescue me, a *sinner*... well, I needed to follow their example. I made up my mind I would live among *Germans*."

All at once, it was so very clear to me. The envelopes, each with ten hundred-dollar bills. "So it was you who gave the money last night!" I blurted out.

He put his finger to his lips and whispered,

"That will be our little secret, Alexander, my friend, ja?"

"Ja," I agreed. But my head was swimming with more questions. "So, what happened to the farmer, Herr Althouse? Did you ever see him again?"

"Oh yes, before I came here I made one last trip to see him. In fact, he gave me this." Mr. Bachman reached into the box, and began squeezing each little sack.

"Ah, here it is." He loosened the cords and withdrew a tiny beautifully-carved figure of baby Jesus. "My rescuer wanted me to have something that would help me remember him... as though I would have ever forgotten him!"

"But Mr. Bachman, I don't get it. You live in this rotten place. You sleep on the floor... when you could live in a mansion. Why?"

"Did Jesus not do much more than this for the world... and for you... and for me... because of love? I think this place is a palace compared to the Bethlehem stable."

The Christmas story suddenly made perfect sense to me.

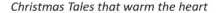

The elderly gentleman sighed, took out his neatly-folded handkerchief, dabbed his eyes and blew his nose.

"So there you have it, Alex, Caroline, and Jo-Jo... your old grandpa is a German, son of a Nazi, saved by a Jew. That's my Christmas story of family secrets!"

"But whatever happened after that?" Caroline asked. "Did your mother get married to Mr. Bachman?"

"Match-making already, are you?" her grandfather laughed. "No, actually, my mother married that pastor I had once very-mistakenly labeled stupid. So I am a preacher's kid, not a diamond dealer!"

"And what about Mr. Bachman? What happened to him?" It was Alex who was asking now.

"Oh, he stayed a few more months in his little apartment and we continued to have wonderful daily talks. He helped me grow in my relationship with Christ and explained lots of Scripture to me. But then he said it was time for him to move on and find another group of "beloved enemies" (as he called them), that he could bless in Jesus' name. So he left New York, but we kept in touch through letters until he passed away many years ago now."

Jo-Jo tapped his grandfather's shoulder impatiently.

"Do you have a picture of him, Grandpa... did he give you any of his diamonds?" It was a run-on question.

Alexander Petersohn lovingly patted his grandson's hand and then struggled stiffly to his feet.

The white-haired grandfather stepped to the middle of the room and looked down at the hodge-podge miniature nativity, so carefully arranged on the coffee table. Then he turned to look intently at each family member for just a moment.

"Remember this Scripture… all of you," he spoke so softly and gently, "… *know the grace of our Lord Jesus Christ, that though he was rich, yet for your sake he became poor, so that you through his poverty might become rich (II Corinthians 8:9).* This is the truth of Christmas and it should not be kept a secret!"

He turned back to his youngest grandchild, his eyes now glistening like the lights on the tree.

"In answer to your question, Jo-Jo… no, I don't have a picture of Mr. Bachman and no, he didn't leave me any gems. But he gave me something much more precious than diamonds…"

Reaching into his jacket pocket he withdrew a beautifully-carved baby Jesus… the same one that appeared magically in the family's manger every Christmas morning.

"Jo-Jo," he sighed and his voice choked as he laid the baby tenderly in the little straw bed, "Mr. Bachman gave me his Jesus."

*Keep on loving one another
as brothers and sisters.
Do not forget to show
hospitality to strangers,
for by so doing some people
have shown hospitality
to angels without knowing it.*

Hebrews 13:1, 2

Christmas at Aunt Allie's

A lex, Caroline and Jo-Jo plunked themselves on the living room floor near their grandfather's feet. Now 15, 13 and 8 respectively, they could no longer crowd onto the overstuffed chair that had become his traditional Christmas Eve throne. Even though they were getting older, they had not outgrown their anticipation of Grandpa's annual Christmas story.

"What are you going to tell us about this year, Grandpa?" Jo-Jo asked eagerly.

The elderly gentleman glanced at his daughter and son-in-law, snuggled close to each other on the couch. The sparkle of the tree lights and crackling flickers from the fireplace created a lovely glow and seemed to spotlight the coffee table in the center of the room. On it was the manger scene... a collection of unusual figurines acquired through the years as gifts or flea market finds. The old man's gaze fixed on the exquisitely-carved figure of baby Jesus and for a moment he seemed to have not heard his grandson's question. But he shook himself back to the present.

"Well, Jo-Jo... you might enjoy hearing from someone else this year." He turned towards the only other

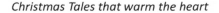
person in the room... a female guest, silver-haired, with an air of gracious elegance, settled comfortably in the wing chair across from him.

"How about it, Ingrid, my little sister... would you tell my family a story?" With a sly grin he continued, "Perhaps your Christmas at Aunt Allie's? You know... the year I was so jealous of you because you got to spend time with our favorite aunt." He gave her a mischievous wink.

"Yeah, go for it!" Alex and Caroline urged. The children were delighted that Aunt Ingrid was with them this year. Now widowed, she had recently returned to the United States from years of missionary service overseas. A visit with her was almost as special as time with their Grandpa.

Ingrid chuckled at her brother's request.

"Oh ja, all right. If you insist. It was after all, a very special Christmas for me."

She folded her hands on her lap and leaned forward as if poised to share with them a very important tale. As it turned out, that's exactly what Alex, Caroline and Jo-Jo were about to hear.

As you know children, I am your grandfather's younger sister. I was born in 1936 in Germany and I'm sure he has told you about our childhood. Our father sent us and Mama to New York to escape the dangers of the second World War. He was a navy doctor and died when the ship he worked on was torpedoed. I think that we would not have survived in New York, if it had not been for the kindness and generosity of our neighbor, Elias Bachman... perhaps your grandpa has told you of him, ja?

(All heads nodded as they recalled the story their grandfather had shared the year before.)

Then you probably also know that our widowed mother ended up marrying the young preacher from our little city church. Eventually our family moved to a rural community in western Pennsylvania where we operated a small business and where our stepfather pastored the only church in town.

Our new papa was kind and loving and, though we missed our own father, Papa Schafer became dear to us. And it was because of him that we met Aunt Allie. She was Papa Schafer's elderly aunt, which made her our great-aunt, just as I am your great-aunt. She lived in Philadelphia.

When I was 16 years-old, Aunt Allie asked me to spend the two weeks preceding Christmas with her.

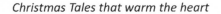

She also invited my parents and brother to drive up on Christmas Eve so we could all enjoy Christmas Day together in the city. My mother tended to be overly-protective... that was understandable, since she had personally experienced much danger and tragedy in her life. She was sure I would be kidnapped or murdered in my sleep by robbers if I visited the big terrible city. Consequently, it took some convincing from Papa that God and Aunt Allie would take good care of me.

Finally, on December 11, 1952, my parents put me on a bus and I was off to Philadelphia.

I felt very grown up travelling on my own. The first part of the trip I daydreamed about living in a big city. I intended to become a fashion designer some day and pictured myself clothing famous people from around the world.

"Although I'll never design for a *German*," I thought. Even though I was a German myself, I had nothing but resentment for that country. I recalled with bitterness all that our family had suffered because folks in my homeland didn't have the courage to stand against evil.

"Nein, nein. No fancy clothes for Germans," I resolved.

As the miles sped past, my thoughts switched to my mother and her reservations about this trip. Perhaps some of her fearfulness had rubbed off on me because, for the rest of the trip, I pictured all kinds of dreadful things which might be awaiting me. Papa always warned me to not let my imagination run wild... but Papa wasn't on the bus.

"I will just have to be very careful," I told myself, "because there are undoubtedly some very bad people in the big city." I remembered stories of murders and crime sprees when we had lived in New York. Philadelphia surely had similar lawlessness. I shivered anxiously.

Finally my thoughts shifted to the holidays. I had been taught that Christmas was the celebration of Jesus' birthday. But I had recently heard in school that no one really knew when Jesus was born. So, though I loved the season's decorations and gifts and parties, I was beginning to wonder if the idea of a baby Savior, announced by an extra-terrestrial chorale to an audience of sheep-herders, wasn't a bit far-fetched. I was kind of glad that I wouldn't have to sit through my Papa's Christmas sermons or participate in a childish pageant again that year.

My great-aunt met me at the station. She was a tiny wisp of a lady with snow white hair that looked like a lily of the valley bloom turned upside down on her head. Though in her 80's, she was spry, spunky, and definitely a no-nonsense kind of person. Her cane, I soon realized, was more for looks than need because I almost had to run to keep up with her.

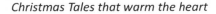

"Come along, Ingrid," she commanded in a voice that my mother said sounded like a smoker's voice. But Papa insisted Aunt Allie never smoked a day in her life. I loved the deep raspy sound and loved even more the permanent twinkle in her eyes. We marched to her home which was only a short distance from the station. As we cut through some back alleys, I kept stealing glances around me, expecting some gangster to accost us at any moment. I was relieved when we passed a police station and Aunt Allie announced that we were almost home. A few more blocks and we arrived.

I had been to Aunt Allie's several years earlier and I wondered if my memory of her home was accurate. As I stood looking at it, I realized the building had not lost a bit of its fascination. It was a charming Victorian house in the heart of the city with a faded "Tourist Home" sign hanging on the front porch rail. Today we would call such a place a "Bed and Breakfast." The old-fashioned title was better suited to Aunt Allie's because she was adamant that she aimed to offer folks much more than just a bed and muffins.

Over the years, she and Uncle Robert had provided a temporary home to hundreds of travelers. But Uncle Bob had passed away, so Aunt Allie was now the sole proprietor. Even before his death, businesses in the heart of the city were fast overtaking the lovely residential area. High-rise hotels had crowded out the more-personal tourist homes. Aunt Allie's three-story abode seemed rather out-of-place, but it was beautiful nonetheless. Lodgers were now rare and, since over the holidays most people went to be with their own families, I expected to have Aunt Allie totally to myself for the next two weeks.

As I stepped into the huge vestibule, I was awe-struck by the amazing old mansion. The curved stair-case led to the second and third floors and finally to the attic. That attic... I remembered it as full of intriguing treasures. The second and third floors each contained three modest-sized bedrooms as well as a "lavatory." Aunt Allie assigned me the bedroom opposite hers on the second floor, so I practically flew up the steps. I dropped my valise in the middle of my room and pounced on the mammoth four-poster bed. But Aunt Allie was calling for me to rejoin her on the first floor, so I scooted back down the steps.

The first floor was magnificent... an elegant parlor and dining room and huge kitchen that smelled of fresh-baked bread. My favorite part of the old house, however, was what Aunt Allie simply called "the back room." Just off the kitchen, the space wasn't much bigger than a large closet and contained only three items. The "morgue slab"... a backless, armless couch, upholstered in a black, scratchy, horse-hair-like fabric... was where Uncle Robert used to take a nap before going to bed

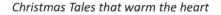
each evening. A concealed pull-out trundle bed was attached beneath it and accommodated extra guests when needed. Beside it was an ancient creaky wooden rocker.

The final fixture in the back room was a large square cage, home to a mischievous-looking smoke-colored bird.

"This is Pilate," Aunt Allie announced. "Uncle Robert and I got him about two years ago, not long before your uncle passed away. He is an African gray and very smart."

"Is he named Pilot because he flies?" I asked.

"Oh no," Aunt Allie corrected me. "His name is spelled P-I-L-A-T-E. Soon after we got him, I became exasperated over a report in the newspaper and I said, 'Honestly Robert, when I read the paper, I just don't know any more what's the truth.' At that moment Pilate (who up to that point had refused to be coaxed into uttering a single word) chimed in, 'What's troot? What's troot? What's troot?' Immediately Robert christened the bird 'Pilate,' after the Roman governor who asked the same question during Jesus' trial. I agreed to the name on the condition that Pilate learn the answer to his own question."

As if to corroborate Aunt Allie's report, Pilate promptly ran through some very spiritual phrases... including "God is goot," "Pray ev'ry day," "Look in da

Book," and "Lord, have mercy!" I was enthralled by the bird and even more amazed when he began crooning the first lines of *Mazin Grace* and *Jeezus Loves Me.*

"Pilate is quite young and capable of learning much more. In fact, that is your first assignment, Ingrid. I want you to teach him some Christmas songs. Now, mind you, no Santa songs," she warned. "Christmas is all about Jesus, not a little round fat man in a red suit. Saint Nicholas was a good Christian man," she declared to me, "and he would not have approved of what we've turned him into. He gave gifts to the poor... needed items, not silly toys and trinkets. Instead of taking their tots to sit on Santa's lap to tell him what they want, parents should send their children to him with gifts to distribute to the homeless. Wouldn't that be a different sight at the department store?"

It was a new thought. Aunt Allie had a way of making me think new thoughts.

"So Pilate needs to sing good traditional carols, although..." she paused, "I do like that song Gene Autry came out with a couple of years ago... *Rudolph, the Red-Nosed Reindeer.* Yes, that would be a fine one to teach Pilate."

I must have looked at her with a shocked expression, because she continued,

"I like that song because there are a lot of outcasts in our world that really have much to offer if we would just give them a chance. We mustn't overlook the friendless. That's a fine Christian message."

So that was that. I had my first assignment from Aunt Allie and I knew she would expect me to do my best in the next two weeks to teach that parrot a Christmas medley.

I did wonder why it was so important for Pilate to learn more music... after all, it was just two of us in the house for Christmas, but I knew better than to argue with my great-aunt.

The next two weeks flew by. I carried armloads of Christmas decorations down from the attic and helped Aunt Allie deck her home from top to bottom with festive Yuletide décor. We headed out into the cold and chose a tall bushy Scotch pine at the Boy Scout stand a few blocks away and then dragged the tree home. I helped Aunt Allie erect it in the parlor and worked with her to adorn it with twinkling lights and exquisite antique ornaments. I trekked with her to Macy's department store and plodded home again with shopping bags full

of gifts… an odd assortment of rather generic but useful items. Of course, she gave me the task of wrapping all of them with the poinsettia-print paper she provided.

My great-aunt's energy level was amazing. I was the teenager with supposedly lots of stamina but she outlasted me every day. In the evenings, Aunt Allie sat in her rocker and I stretched out on the morgue slab while she told me stories from her past. They were far more fascinating than any radio or TV show. Then she would read while I repeated the first line of *Joy to the World*, and *Rudolph, the Red-nosed Reindeer* over and over and over again to her pet bird. But Pilate remained stubbornly silent. I was becoming weary of the job but Aunt Allie refused to let me quit.

Three days before Christmas, we tackled the baking. I mixed and rolled, cut, sprinkled, and iced dozens of cookies. We made tarts, fancy breads, and gallons of soup to put in Aunt Allie's icebox. I couldn't believe the amount of food she was preparing. Who was going to eat all this stuff? I had a healthy appetite but there was no way my family and I could devour the mounds of food we had prepared.

Two days before Christmas, I finally got up the nerve to ask the question that had been on my mind for days.

"Aunt Allie, we've done all this cooking and cleaning and decorating and gift-buying… but why? It will

just be you and me and Papa and Mama and Alex for Christmas. We have enough stuff to entertain an army for Christmas."

She laughed and tapped her cane on the floor. "Don't you worry, Ingrid. Sometimes I just feel God wants me to get ready for something or someone. I don't usually know the details, just that I'm to get ready. So that's what we've been doing. I'm convinced there's also a reason why God brought you here to help me this year. There's something very special for you this Christmas, I'm certain. Just you wait and see."

I went to bed that night wondering about what Aunt Allie had said. I had worked very hard for the last two weeks, doing whatever Aunt Allie had requested. Some of it had been fun but a lot of it had been plain hard work. Now that everything was finished, I realized I wasn't feeling much anticipation. Maybe I was outgrowing the childish excitement of Christmas. Maybe my doubts about God and Jesus were stealing my Christmas joy. Maybe I was just tired. I fell asleep in a not-so-celebratory mood. Still, what was it Aunt Allie had said? "Something very special about this Christmas..." I was doubtful, but then again, maybe she knew something I didn't.

December 24 began with a crimson sunrise. Aunt Allie was already in the kitchen when I descended for breakfast.

"This is the day!" She greeted me enthusiastically. But I was not feeling very merry. Still, Papa and Mama and Alex would arrive that evening and that was kind of special.

As I was finishing breakfast, I looked out the window just in time to see the sun disappear behind a gigantic wall of menacing clouds.

"Whoa, looks like snow, Aunt Allie. Maybe we'll have a white Christmas."

"Yes, Ingrid, we just might!" She chuckled softly. It sounded a little eerie, actually.

By mid-morning, I knew that we were in for much more than a white Christmas. We were in for a blizzard! The phone in the front hallway rang. It was Papa calling to say there was no way the family would be able to make the trip to Philadelphia. Roads were already becoming unpassable.

"Nothing special about this Christmas," I thought. "We did all that work. I slaved for my ancient relative, and now I won't even get to spend Christmas with my family!" I figured I'd be penned up with Aunt Allie for days and probably have to shovel tons of snow. How quickly I had gone from wanting to be in the city to longing for escape from it.

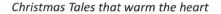

By suppertime I was just plain glum. Aunt Allie was humming Christmas carols and seemed oblivious to the fact that my Christmas was going to be boring. Suddenly Aunt Allie tapped her cane and said,

"Cheer up, Ingrid! You mustn't give up on God. He can always do more than what we expect. You must trust Him. He really does care about each one of us, you know."

I doubted that. After all I wasn't sure I even believed all the "Christian stuff" anymore. But Aunt Allie seemed so totally confident.

"Well God," I prayed silently, "looks like I'm stuck in this house with tons of food and presents and only an old lady and a parrot for company. If You really do exist (and I'm not convinced You do), I can't imagine how You could salvage this Christmas, but it sure would be nice if You would do something to make things a little more fun."

I went to the parlor to mope and wait for Christmas.

The procession started at 7 o'clock.

Footsteps clomping on the porch and a knock on the front door. Aunt Allie was there quick as a wink, and I was right behind her. A tall skinny man with thick-lensed black-rimmed glasses introduced himself as Mr. Fierstein. His hair and jacket were coated with snow.

"I'm so sorry to intrude on Christmas Eve," he spoke through chattering teeth. "I walked from the station. None of the buses are running due to the storm, so I'm in a predicament."

"I'm sure you're not the only one," Aunt Allie smiled and pulled him into the hallway. "Welcome to Aunt Allie's!"

He was a kind of shifty-looking character and I hung a little closer to Aunt Allie. She assigned him to the third-floor bedroom right above mine.

Next came a rough-looking couple. The man was huge and intimidating, in a black leather jacket, black jeans, and boots with silver toes that appeared potentially lethal. He had what looked like one of Papa's red work handkerchiefs tied on his head and greasy hair hanging on his shoulders. His slinky girlfriend had the same ugly skull and snake design on her jacket.

"This d**n sh*ty weather is messin' up our plans big time! My name's Lion and this here's my girlfriend, Weasel. You got a place we can crash?"

"Young man, the weather is neither cursed nor excremental! The good Lord sends the snow and always for a reason, one of which is evidently to bring you here. Of course I have a place for you!"

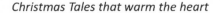

In spite of my fear of being housed with this pair, I had to smile when Aunt Allie led them to the back bedroom on the third floor… the only one with two single beds. I might have been a naïve country kid but I knew something about morality. Aunt Allie was pretty shrewd.

About 30 minutes later, Dede arrived, a ditsy blonde cocktail waitress that couldn't get her car to start when she left the bar to head home. Mama would have said she had a trashy mouth but it was just the big wad of chewing gum she chomped on with lips wide apart. Her dress was short at both the bottom and the top and she was a little too chunky to make either end look good. Dede was installed on the second floor, in the room between Aunt Allie's and mine. Her cheap perfume smelled kind of like wet hay bales. It started to give me a headache.

Nevertheless, I would have taken Dede's aroma any day over the final guest's. Tony was a grimy shoe-shine guy who looked like he hadn't shaved in days and smelled like he hadn't bathed in weeks. I was horrified when Aunt Allie enthusiastically offered him the final third-floor bedroom.

I couldn't imagine what we would do with these bizarre guests for the next few days and the thought of sleeping under the same roof with them terrified me. I could now understand why my mother was nervous about me coming to the city. Instead of special, the situation was now downright *scary*. But Aunt Allie was unflustered.

"I'd like us all to gather in the parlor at 9:30," she announced to each one as they arrived. "This is Christmas Eve and God has brought you all here for a very special Christmas celebration."

None of them looked very impressed. But amazingly, at 9:30, they were all seated in the beautifully-decorated parlor, looking weary, wary and not very warm towards me or my elderly aunt.

"Friends," Aunt Allie began, "you may think of me as just an old lady who happened to be at the right place at the right time for all of you. But I want you to know that I am a Christian and so I believe it's no accident that you're here. God brought you. I want you to enjoy your stay and I also want you to understand, before you leave, that God loves you very, very much."

Without waiting for any response, she proceeded to open her Bible and explain the Christmas story in the most down-to-earth way I had ever heard. I watched our guests. They seemed to be paying attention.

"It doesn't matter, dear friends, who we are, where we are from, or how good or bad we've been... not one of us has any hope of getting into heaven without help. Jesus Christ came to make a way. That is the message of Christmas!"

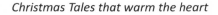

As Aunt Allie concluded her little talk, everyone sat in a kind of reverent hush, almost like in church. Suddenly the silence was pierced by a loud cackle from the back room. It was Pilate... singing... well not a song really... a measly three-note refrain with one repeating word....

"Wudolf! Wudolf! Wudolf!" With uncanny timing, he chose that moment to finally show off one of the carols I had worked so hard to teach him.

Everyone in the parlor burst out laughing and all at once I was hit with an amazing realization. Before me was a room full of Rudolphs! And my Aunt saw something good in each of them. But... they still made me uneasy!

Pilate's interruption transformed the atmosphere. Before I knew it, Dede and Weasel were helping Aunt Allie fill trays with the goodies we had made that week. The three men were spreading out a 1000-piece jigsaw puzzle on the dining table. The rest of the evening began to seem more like a celebration. Dede and Weasel turned out to be pretty handy in the kitchen, which gave me a break. Lion called me "Goofus" and I didn't know whether that meant he liked me or hated me. Mr. Fierstein actually told a couple of not-half-bad jokes. Even Tony didn't smell as bad when surrounded by the scent of cinnamon, cloves, and nutmeg.

When we finally retired to our bedrooms around 11, I snuggled under my comforter and reviewed the events

of the evening. I recalled how Aunt Allie had repeatedly called her guests, "friends," and treated them like she really meant that. The scripture she had read came back to me, "Greater love has no man than this, that a man lay down his life for his friends."

I knew my definition of "friend" was much different from Aunt Allie's. I still viewed the assortment of travelers as suspicious... not quite as bad as Germans, but pretty close. I would be glad when the blizzard was over and they would all be gone and I could return home. Still, Pilate's "Wudolf" was almost too coincidental to be a coincidence. I yawned and, thinking of friends and enemies, drifted off to sleep.

At midnight I heard Aunt Allie's cane-clonking steps descending to the front door. I jumped out of bed and opened the iron grate on my bedroom floor, through which I could see right into the front hallway.

"Oh no, more visitors!" I sighed.

Of course, Aunt Allie was ushering the pair right in. I recognized the garb immediately... a young Amish couple. I was from western Pennsylvania but I was familiar with the religious group that lived very simply. I pressed my ear against the open vent and gathered bits of their conversation. Like our other guests, their bus had been cancelled and someone at the station had suggested they try finding a place at Aunt Allie's. I didn't know where in the world Aunt Allie would put them, since the bedrooms were all taken but, in true Christmas fashion, my innkeeper aunt led them to where else, but the back room.

At this point, Jo-Jo, who liked to think he was a step ahead of everyone else, interrupted Aunt Ingrid.

"Oh... and I bet the Amish lady was pregnant and had a baby and they all sang, *We Wish You a Merry Christmas!*" He laughed and looked expectantly around the room.

"Shush, Jo-Jo!" Alex scolded. "Don't be so rude. Aunt Ingrid's not finished."

The story-teller smiled patiently.

"Actually, Jo-Jo...you're partly right. The lady was pregnant although, believe it or not, I didn't even know what that word meant in those days. With her loose-fitting cape dress, I never suspected anything out of the ordinary. All I knew was that the young couple was soon settled with the parrot in the back room and Aunt Allie was plodding upstairs to her room. I climbed into bed and fell asleep."

Around 3 a.m. I was awakened again, this time by many footsteps in the hall. I slid groggily from my bed and crept to the door, cracking it a sliver, just in time to see Lion and Weasel carrying a large wooden chest down the stairs. Next came Dede, a heavy-looking box in her arms. Aunt Allie followed. Although, to my sleepy brain, it appeared she was being roughly driven by Mr. Fierstein and Tony who were right behind her, also with arms filled with "loot" from the attic.

In my semi-conscious state and perhaps fueled by my wild imagination and my mother's fears, I knew immediately what was happening. Aunt Allie was being taken hostage and our house guests were ganging together to rob her!

Summoning the little courage I had, I donned my robe and sneaked down the stairs, keeping far enough back from my great-aunt's captors that no one would detect me. When the procession reached the first floor, it headed towards the kitchen.

"Of course," I reasoned, "they will lock Aunt Allie in the back room with that poor unsuspecting Amish pair." I figured the young religious couple couldn't be in on this evil plot.

"They'll come for me next and then they will ransack the whole house," I concluded, now in a panic. I heard pots and pans rattling in the kitchen and the door of the back room slam.

When I reached the vestibule, I pressed against the wall and tried to see what was going on in the kitchen. Tony and Mr. Fierstein were opening and closing cupboards, undoubtedly looking for more valuables. I couldn't see anyone else. Tiptoeing to the phone on the table in the foyer, I grabbed the whole contraption and slipped into the hallway closet. I hoped the thieves wouldn't notice the cord leading to my hiding spot. I dialed "0" and prayed to the God I wasn't sure existed.

"Please let someone answer!" I pleaded.

Within minutes, I had relayed our desperate situation to the Operator who assured me that police would be contacted immediately. From the closet, I scurried to the parlor and hid behind the floor-length satin draperies where, through the front window, I would be able to see an approaching police car.

Only then did I realize that no cars were driving

anywhere. The snow was still falling and already close to two feet had accumulated.

"Oh no," I thought. "We're doomed!" I could hear ominous sounds coming from the back of the house... items being slid across the floor, groans and Aunt Allie's voice...

"God help us!" If Aunt Allie was afraid, I knew the situation had to be truly serious. Even Pilate was screeching out, "Lord have mercy! Lord have mercy! Lord have mercy!" That parrot seemed almost human.

Then peering back out the front window, I saw a welcome sight... two policemen, on foot, trudging towards me through the snow. I scooted to the front door and eased it open for my snow-covered saviors. One looked young and handsome and the other old and experienced, but what I liked best were the guns in their holsters.

In a whisper, I updated them as to what was happening and, with weapons drawn, they crept back the hallway towards the kitchen. They commanded me to stay in the parlor but I figured the safest place in the house at that moment was right behind them, so I followed closely.

What happened next took only seconds but, to me, it seemed like a slow-motion film. Mr. Fierstein and

Tony almost fainted from fright and surprise when the two cops appeared in the kitchen, pointing their guns and ordering them to get their hands in the air. The two complied in stunned shock.

Then the older cop put his hand on the doorknob to the back room and, like you see the modern S.W.A.T. teams do, burst into the small room where the hostages were being held.

"Police!" he shouted. "Don't anyone move!"

"Well, Hallelujah! Thank You Jesus!" I heard Aunt Allie exclaim. Suddenly her cane hooked around the cop's wrist and he was being yanked into the room by my feisty great-aunt who was now acting like his commander-in-chief.

"I certainly hope you do know how to deliver a baby!"

And so, with an audience of peculiar people and competent assistance from two capable law enforcement officers, the young Amish woman delivered her babies... yes, not just one but *two*...a little boy and a little girl!

The motley gang of guests congratulated each other as though the babies belonged to them! Dede and Weasel oohed and aahed over the twins. Tony and Mr. Fierstein shook hands with everyone. Lion and the young police-man gave each other friendly slaps on the back. What an unlikely friendship... all because of these babies.

I was totally embarrassed by my wrong assumptions, but everyone laughed and assured me that my imagination had actually saved the day. I looked around the little room, now a nursery, transformed by the many attic treasures our guests had lugged down at Aunt Allie's bidding only a few hours earlier.

The parents cradled their infants and Aunt Allie laid her hands tenderly on each child. Then, in her raspy voice, she began a prayer of blessing over those precious children born Christmas morning. There wasn't a single dry eye in that back room when she pronounced the "Amen."

Then, in true Pilate unpredictability, the gray parrot began to sing the other song I had worked so hard to teach him,

"Joy tooda World! Joy tooda World! Lord iz cum! Lord iz cum!" We all laughed with real tears of joy trickling down our cheeks.

"What a special Christmas!" I told myself. "What do you know? God certainly did answer my request to brighten up Christmas. I guess He really does love everyone... even me." In that moment, my doubts disappeared like a puff of smoke, never to return.

I was never the same after my Christmas at Aunt Allie's. And to this day, it is my very favorite Christmas memory!

The three children sighed contentedly.

"That was really amazing, Aunt Ingrid!" Caroline was the first to speak. "Thank you so much for telling us. But I'm curious. Do you know what happened to any of those people?"

"Oh, Aunt Allie kept in contact with all of them. They exchanged Christmas cards every year and I know that some, if not all of them, put their trust in Jesus, in large part because of the gracious kindness and clear explanations from my great-aunt."

"I'm sure it made quite an impression on the policemen as well," Alex added.

"Yes it did and Aunt Allie kept in contact with them too. In fact," she added as a tender tear began to glisten in her eye, "that young policeman got my name and address from Aunt Allie. We began corresponding and eventually he became my husband!"

Gasps erupted from the three youngsters.

"Whoa... but I thought you married a missionary, Aunt Ingrid!" Jo-Jo had finally met his match for surprise endings.

"That Christmas at Aunt Allie's so impacted us that we felt the Lord calling us to share His good news full-time in another country. Instead of becoming a fashion designer for the rich and famous, my husband and I went to the poor and needy. And, of course, it probably will come as no surprise at all that God called us to do that in Germany!"

"Children," Aunt Ingrid looked intently at the three. "Remember this: the story of Christmas is all about God caring enough for the poor and needy of the world... and that includes all of us... that He opened His home and heart to them. That is news worth sharing!"

Without a word, the children's elderly grandpa struggled to his feet and disappeared down the hallway, returning in a moment carrying what looked to be a large box, covered with a sheet.

He set it on the coffee table by the manger and, with a dramatic flourish, pulled back the cloth.

There, blinking impishly at the family with its now 66-year-old eyes and puffing up its smoke-colored feathers, was Pilate. With the Christmas lights suddenly rousing him and Aunt Ingrid coaxing him, to the delight of the whole family, he began chirping his Christmas medley... now practiced over years and years.

"So you see my dear nephews and niece," Ingrid added merrily above Pilate's screeching melodies, "I not only inherited a great faith from Aunt Allie... I inherited her parrot!"

*Beyond all question,
the mystery from which
true godliness springs is great...*

1 Timothy 3:16

The Journal

"What's that ugly old book doing on the coffee table?"

Mug of steaming cocoa in hand, Caroline had just entered the tree-lit parlor, eager for her family's yearly Christmas Eve gathering. At 14, she already had a well-developed taste for tidy and the worn, tattered-edge album seemed out-of-place beside the lovely nativity scene so neatly arranged in the center of the table.

"I'll move it!" Her older brother Alex grabbed the book and, with three-pointer precision, lobbed it toward the corner of the room. It dropped with a thud on the carpet.

"No!" a much-too-stern-for-Christmas voice commanded.

The children's father, Jason Sherman, pushed roughly past his son and knelt to retrieve the tossed-aside volume. Tenderly he cradled it, returning to his wife Laura at their favorite end of the sofa. Across the room, his elderly father-in-law was already seated on his throne... an oversized wing chair with the youngest member of the family straddling the upholstered arm. Jo, now proud to be a mature nine-year-old, had recently graduated from "Jo-Jo" to just "Jo" but he had not yet abandoned his favorite seat next to his silver-haired grandfather.

"Grandpa," Jo began, "what's your story going to be about?"

For many years, Alexander Petersohn had entertained and inspired the family with his tales and they had become a much-anticipated Christmas tradition.

"Actually," the old man replied. "I asked your father to share a story this year."

A groan erupted simultaneously from the three children. Kind-hearted Caroline tried to soften the blow.

"No offense, Dad... but we do listen to you every Sunday in church, as well as at our midweek service."

"No offense taken. I understand it must at times get tiresome being a pastor's kids. But last week, I finally decided to go through a carton of books I inherited from my parents. It's been stashed in the attic for years. I assumed it was just a bunch of old junk. But when I started digging through the box, I discovered... this!" Jason patted the leather cover of the large book he had just rescued.

"What I found inside... well, to me it was like finding a priceless buried treasure. It is an album, a journal of sorts... compiled by my father over many years. It includes quotes, newspaper clippings, poems, and personal diary-type entries that shed light on my past and, more importantly, your grandfather's past. This is your history too. So I thought I would share some of it with you children tonight... particularly a few very special entries. You won't be disappointed."

"Go for it Dad." Alex encouraged. And Jo piped in,

"Yeah Daddy... we're all ears!"

Jason opened the precious volume and flipped through the first yellowed pages.

As I was growing up in a small community in the foothills of the Colorado Rockies, some of my friends would tease me about my parents. Tatti (as I called my father) and Mame (as I called my mother) had much grayer hair than my friends' parents. And they talked with a very different accent than my friends' parents.

"Tatti" and "Mame" are actually Yiddish names for "father"' and "mother." My parents were immigrants. I would describe Tatti as a Polish version of Tevye from Fiddler on the Roof.

One day, when I was about five, one of my buddies came up to me, jabbed his finger against my chest and announced,

"Your parents aren't really your parents, you know."

I was confused and embarrassed and ran home crying.

I remember Tatti picked me up in his strong arms, put his bristly cheek against mine and said,

"We are your parents, Jason. You just didn't come to us the same way that most children come."

He proceeded to tell me that my first parents had died and that he and Mame had become my parents right around my second birthday.

"So, we *are* your parents," Tatti assured me, "just Parents Number Two!"

That was that. It was a good enough explanation for me. In later years, they filled in more details about "Parents Number One," as they called them but, at five years of age, all I needed to know was that Tatti and Mame were indeed my father and mother.

But here's what I discovered in this book... a newspaper clipping from 1972. The headline reads, "Local couple dies in tragic car accident. Toddler son to be adopted by local veterinarian and wife." Below the article, in Tatti's handwriting, is this:

Today, I, Josef Sherman, became Tatti.
And my beloved Ester is finally Mame! How can
such joy come from such sadness? Our young
neighbors did not deserve to die. But now at
45 years of age, unable to have children... we
have a son! As my own father told me years
ago in Poland, "With a child in the house, all
corners are full." Yes, our corners are full.
Jason! Our Jason... one boy... such joy!

I always knew Tatti loved me but, somehow, reading
that entry made me feel all warm inside. Tatti wasn't
one to talk a lot about his feelings. He was pretty much
a no-nonsense, matter-of-fact kind of guy. But this
book is giving me a glimpse of the deep emotion that he
harbored inside.

When I was 10, I witnessed first-hand Tatti's usually-
hidden tender side. Now let me see... where is that entry?

Jason turned a few pages and then smiled as he
spied what he was looking for.)

Yes. Here it is. But you need a little background first...

I often went along with Tatti on his vet calls. The
farmers in the area depended on him to care for their
sick animals and he was always willing to help, no
matter what time of day or night he was called.

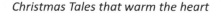

One early December evening, I accompanied him to a sheep farmer's ranch. Their Shetland sheepdog was having trouble whelping the last of her pups. Tatti worked patiently, his large hands soothing the nervous mother and working to free the little puppy. When the pup was finally delivered, it was obvious he was much smaller than the rest of the litter and barely breathing. The farmer declared he had no time to deal with "the runt"' so Tatti wrapped him up and we brought him home. For hours, Tatti sat by our fireplace cradling that tiny Sheltie. He fed him milk with an eye-dropper. He gently massaged his back and belly. I remember Mame asking Tatti a couple of times why he didn't just give up and let the dog die. But Tatti said, "my father used to say… 'as long as one limb stirs, one does not think of the grave.'"

Tatti called the pup "Bissel," because that was Yiddish for "a little bit" and that was exactly what he was… just a little bit of a dog. When I was not at school, I spelled Tatti off and, between the two of us, we nursed that puppy to health. By the time Christmas Eve arrived, I was tremendously attached to the dog. I begged Tatti to let me keep him. But Tatti said he didn't belong to us and that the farmer would get a good price for a purebred Sheltie, even if he was 'a little bissel.' He turned and walked out of the house with the precious puppy tucked snugly in a small basket. He was delivering him back to his owner. Tatti appeared unmoved by my pleading and I went to bed that Christmas Eve, crying and angry. I awoke Christmas morning still in the depths of despair and aching with the pain of loss. But when I finally came down to the kitchen for breakfast, there was the little basket by my plate.

Tatti simply said, "The farmer had no interest in the runt. He's yours if you want him."

Such delight after such disappointment. I danced around the room with excitement, cuddling the little pup in my arms!

Bissel was really Tatti's dog as well as mine. When I arrived from school each day, the little sheep dog would come running, jumping up and acting like his long-lost friend had returned. And he rescued me more than once from dangerous scrapes I got myself into... like the time I fell into the creek and Bissel dragged me out. I loved that dog! But during the day while I was at school, Bissel was Tatti's shadow... trotting behind him to his vet calls, perching beside him in the front seat of our old pick-up truck, and curling up on the sofa beside Tatti every night after I went to bed.

Now, here's what I discovered in Tatti's book:

So my boy wants a dog... he thinks he will enjoy life more with a dog. He doesn't know yet that life is so full of troubles. What

good will a dog do? Just more trouble, if you ask me. And yet... as my father used to say, 'Troubles with soup is easier than troubles without soup.' Maybe troubles with a dog would be easier than troubles without a dog. But that greedy farmer wants a small fortune for this dog that he was willing to let die just a few weeks ago. Better that man's teeth should all fall out but one... just to make him suffer. Well, I was planning to put a new heater in my truck but I guess I can wear an extra pair of long johns for another winter... because a Bissell for my boy is just a bissel I can do for one I love so much!

So I got a dog and Tatti suffered through another cold winter in his drafty old truck. I always wondered why he didn't get that heater fixed. Now I know.

About two years after that, Tatti and I had our first serious theological discussion. Mame took me to church, for as long as I can remember. The little Baptist chapel in town preached salvation and sanctification but it was my mother who taught me about Jesus and

His love. Tatti once said that "one mother achieves more than a hundred teachers," and that was certainly true of Mame. She was wiser than many Bible scholars. I never understood why Tatti didn't go along with us to church. I dared to ask him only a few times. Mostly he just shrugged and changed the subject. One time he said, "Every man has his burden" and turned his face away. Another time he said, "If it would help to pray to God, then people would be hiring others to pray for them."

But he never seemed to mind that Mame and I went to church or that Mame prayed faithfully at every meal and at bed time. He even went along with us to church for special occasions like Christmas or Easter... yet he seemed untouched by any talk about God.

One hot summer afternoon, I was helping Tatti split wood out behind our house. We were both tired and almost suffocating from the heat and humidity. Even Bissel had quit his usual racing around and had plopped down, panting under the shade of a large maple.

Tatti's usual wardrobe was a long-sleeved flannel shirt and blue jeans and it didn't seem to matter what the temperature was... this was what he wore. But this particular day was so sweltering hot and, for the first time I could remember, Tatti unbuttoned and removed his sweat-soaked shirt, revealing a thin undershirt below. That's when I noticed the black letter and numbers on the inner side of his left upper forearm.

"Tatti... what is that on your arm?" I asked. "A tattoo? I didn't think you liked tattoos."

At first I thought he didn't hear me.

"Tatti," I persisted. "What are all those numbers?"

He kept swinging his axe and I was about to ask a third time, when he straightened up and turned to face me. His eyes were hard and, in a tone I had never heard from him before, he almost hissed his reply.

"That Jason, is the combination to the gate of *hell!*"

The venom in his voice shocked me. He continued.

"That is why I don't pray, Jason. I am a Polish Jew. I was raised to believe in God. But then the war came." His voice quieted and he stared off in the distance for a moment. "Every heart has its secrets, Jason. Every man has his burden. But I have carried burdens more than many men. I was a prisoner of war, Jason. I lost my..." he paused and when he continued his voice trembled... "my father and my mother and my little brother. I still believe in God... but I do not understand Him, Jason. You and Ester say such good things about your Jesus but they are just words to me. When there is bitterness in the heart, sugar in the mouth won't make life sweeter."

Tatti wiped his brow and it looked to me like he wiped the corners of his eyes as well. Then he swung the axe into a log and I knew our discussion was over.

I couldn't get up the nerve to speak of what he suffered for several years. And Tatti never brought it up either. But, in this book, I discovered much more than Tatti ever shared with me.

(Jason turned the album around to reveal a page of horrifying newspaper articles.)

"Approximately 6 million Jews killed in Europe. 91% of Polish Jews, three million men, women and children murdered at hands of Nazis."

I had studied about the holocaust in history class but, as I read these articles, I was sickened. And Tatti's entry broke my heart even more:

Auschwitz... such horrors I saw there... such horrors were done to me there. Every day, death and suffering and cruelty all around me... and no escape. Evil. Such unspeakable evil! Then... January 1945... herded up like sheep and made to walk for days... the "death march," we called it. People dropped like flies on every side of me. Barely allowed to stop and rest but, when we did, we slept in ditches in the bitter cold. I wasn't sure I still

believed in God and yet I asked for His mercy. No, I didn't ask. I begged for His mercy!

One frigid morning I awoke. The two men on either side of me were dead. I survived because I was in the warmer spot between them. I took their shirts. Those tattered shirts saved me from freezing.

And then the convoy... American servicemen... young men just like me. Had they seen horrors like me? I hoped not. They were my rescuers, my saviors! I was finally free and yet... still a prisoner to the nightmares in my soul.

God! So many, many died! Yet I survived.

It is a mystery I cannot explain!

"Daddy, this is so sad. This is not a happy Christmas story at all," Caroline chided.

"You're right. It is very sad," Jason replied. "But I think it is important that we never forget that, without God, there is great evil in the world. I promise the story will get better."

After Tatti told me that little bit about his war experience, I went to Mame and she filled in a lot more of the details. Yes, he was rescued by the U.S. convoy and taken to a refugee camp. That is where he met Mame. She was a survivor from Treblinka, a prison camp near Warsaw. She was 16 at the time. Tatti was 18. They became friends and were soon married by an army chaplain. He helped them get visas and passage to the United States. It was also because of him that Mame gave her life to Jesus. She told me that it was only because of Jesus that she was able to heal from the traumas of what she had suffered.

But Tatti just couldn't seem to take that step of faith. The chaplain was from Colorado and knew a sheep rancher who could use a farm hand. Tatti had always liked animals, so he took the job.

After arriving in New York, they took the train west. Tatti did so well with the animals that his employer helped him get some training so he could begin working as a vet. You already know how I happened to become their son and they became Parents Number Two.

Anyway, after that stifling day when Tatti revealed his past to me, I became determined to *make* him become a Christian. Throughout my teen years, I talked to him about Jesus every opportunity I could. He usually got quiet... sometimes he gave an angry sigh and stomped away. Why couldn't I get through to him? He was wise in so many ways. How could he be so blind to God's love?

Then came December, 1990. I was 20 and had just finished my first term at seminary. I headed home for the holidays, feeling a tremendous urgency to convince Tatti of the truth of the gospel. Mame and I had prayed for this stubborn guy for so many years and still he seemed unmoveable. He was now 63 years old and, to me, that seemed to be getting dangerously old. (By the way... now it doesn't seem nearly so old.) I often reminded God that time was running out.

On Christmas Eve, the three of us attended the service at our little country church. The sanctuary was beautifully decorated. Candles glimmered at the windows. Pine scent filled the air. Tatti sat stoic throughout all the lovely carols. The pastor spoke of Christmas dreams... how God used a dream to reassure Joseph that he should go ahead and marry his young sweetheart. He used a dream to warn the wise men of danger so they could escape Herod. And He used a dream to warn Joseph to escape with Mary and baby

Jesus to Egypt. I kept sneaking sideways looks at Tatti. Untouched, as usual. I loved my father so much but I felt helpless to free him from the pain of his past.

When we arrived home, Bissel greeted us with all the enthusiasm a now-15-year-old Sheltie could muster. Mame started putting the final touches on goodies for Christmas morning. Tatti and I settled ourselves with books, on either side of the fireplace. Bissel curled up at Tatti's feet. Outside, snow had begun falling. The forecast was predicting over a foot by morning. It would have been a picture-postcard Christmas Eve setting, except for the frustration that churned in me. Finally, I couldn't stand it any longer.

"Tatti," I erupted. "What keeps you from trusting Jesus as your Savior?" Thinking back, I must admit my tone was not a gentle "Just As I Am" invitation. It was an exasperated accusation.

He sat silent for a moment and then looked at me sadly.

"It is the evil, Jason... so much evil that I saw... and *still* see. I have no explanation for it. Neither do you. The eggs are not smarter than the chickens... you're just an egg, Jason."

I exploded back, "You're right Tatti. I *am* just an egg and I don't have a perfect explanation for the terrible tragedy in this world. It is a mystery. A big mystery! I don't have all the theological answers you want. But I know one thing… we would not even recognize evil, unless goodness existed. The bad… I don't pretend to understand why it happens or what causes it. But I have seen that God is powerful enough and kind enough and interested enough to bring good out of the worst things that happen to us. To me, that is a much bigger and amazing mystery! Think about it, Tatti…" (By then, I was shouting at him.) "If you hadn't gone through Auschwitz, you wouldn't have met Mame. If those men hadn't died beside you in the ditch, you wouldn't have lived. If those young soldiers hadn't been sent to war, you would never have been rescued. And Tatti, if my Parents Number One hadn't died, I would never have gained Parents Number Two! I wouldn't have become your son. I would never have come to love you so much!"

At that point, tears were streaming down my face and I couldn't say any more. I stormed down the hall to my bedroom, slamming the door behind me. How could Tatti be so stubborn and blind? I flopped on my bed, discouraged and mad and incredibly sad. I fell asleep definitely not thinking of sugar plums but questioning if God could ever crack a hard nut like Tatti.

I awakend to Mame shaking me.

"Jason, wake up! I think something has happened to your father." I sat up immediately.

"Why Mame? Where is he? "I struggled to rub the sleep from my eyes.

"Right after you went to bed last night, he got a call from our neighbor... something about a ewe and a sickly lamb. So, of course, your father headed out with Bissel. I figured it was taking longer than usual but you know sometimes complications arise. Jason, Bissel just came to the door and he's bleeding and Tatti's not with him. I called the farmer and he said Tatti left his place soon after midnight. That was hours ago! You know that farm's only a few miles away. He should have been home ages ago."

I looked at my dog... whimpering and already tugging on the leg of my pajamas. "Oh God, please!" I whispered. "Let Tatti be safe!"

The next hours were a blur. We called the police, but I wasn't about to wait around for their arrival. I knew the roads would slow them down terribly. As fast as I could, I bandaged Bissel's wounds, thanking God they weren't too deep. I donned snow shoes and headed out to find Tatti. I decided to take a short-cut across the pastures.

"Bissel, take me to him, buddy!"

Even though the neighbor's place wasn't far, I knew there was a pretty steep stretch of road between our properties and Tatti was still driving that rattle-trap of a pickup with bald tires. I feared the worst.

In spite of his age and injuries, Bissell ran ahead of me through the drifts, obviously knowing right where he was headed. It was slow going, as I trekked across the fields. The whole time, I kept replaying the angry words I had spewed at Tatti the night before. I pleaded with Jesus to let him be okay.

Well, we found him but, as I feared… at the bottom of the steep ravine. The pickup had slid off the road and tumbled down the embankment. He was pinned behind the steering wheel, a nasty gash on his head. He was breathing, barely. Dog hair and blood spatter on the jagged glass of a smashed passenger window revealed Bissel's escape route.

The emergency crew arrived shortly and those guys worked feverishly to free Tatti. How they ever managed to get him out and onto a stretcher…. and then how they carried him back up that snow-covered bank, I'll never understand.

It wasn't long until the ambulance was headed to the hospital, sirens blaring and lights flashing.

Definitely not the kind of Christmas sounds and lights I had expected for that day. A state trooper offered to take me right to the hospital but I asked him instead to drop Bissel and me back at the house so I could get Mame. I could drive her to the hospital in my own car. Besides, I was formulating a plan that I was pretty sure would not fly with the policeman.

My old gym bag was just the right size and Bissel seemed to grasp immediately what I had in mind. He hopped into the bag. I zipped it shut except for a small space for air and thanked God that Bissel was the runt of the litter. Mame and I and my stow-away headed to the hospital.

The doctor that greeted us had grim news. The combination of Tatti's injury, the cold temperatures, and shock had left him in critical condition. He told me my father was unlikely to survive the day.

"Oh no, Daddy! You mean Tatti died on Christmas Day?" It was Jo interrupting this time. "I won't ever like Christmas again!"

"Hold on a bit longer," his dad urged. "I thought just like you, Jo. It was bad enough that Tatti lay dying in a hospital bed but, on top of that, it was Christmas! I just couldn't understand the events that were swirling around me. But the story's not over yet."

I remember Mame stroking Tatti's face. She leaned close to his ear and whispered her love to him. It brought tears to my eyes. But finally I insisted she sit and rest. She had been up most of the night and was obviously exhausted.

When I was sure the coast was clear, I unzipped my bag and lifted my passenger out. I nestled Bissel under the sheet, right beside Tatti. I lifted Tatti's dead weight of a hand and placed it on Bissel's soft fur. Bissel looked up at me, his big brown eyes full of concern for his master. To my horror, the doctor walked in right then and stopped abruptly when he spied a sheep dog in his patient's bed.

"Please, Doc" I begged. "He will be Tatti's best medicine."

The doctor hesitated and then, as if not wanting to incriminate himself by sticking around, turned and left the room without a word. I sat across from our dog and took the other hand of the man I felt helpless to save.

"So did he live, Dad?" This time it was Alex. "He didn't die then, did he?"

Jason turned a few more pages in the time-worn book.

"No, he didn't die that Christmas Day. Let me read to you Tatti's own words scribbled on a hospital note-pad, soon after he awoke on December 27, 1992..."

Well I gave them all quite a scare. I didn't plan to slide off the road and end up at the bottom of that gully. I remember thinking, "Here I am... once again in a ditch, on a cold, dark night. And once again, I doubt that I'll make it out alive."

But I did.

"It's a mystery!" Those were Jason's words. Ah... my son was mad like a bull when he said that. But he was right. So many puzzles with no easy answers. A lamb died. I couldn't save it. Yet, I was saved. I will live, I think. And I'm glad I will. Maybe Jason and Ester have been right all along. Maybe it is because we have tasted the bitter that we can finally savor the sweet. Maybe it is only

when there seems no escape that we look for rescue. Maybe because of sin, there must be a Savior.

Of course, at the time, I didn't know he wrote this. Apparently he jotted those words when Mame and I were out of his room. He was only awake for a few short hours and then he took a turn for the worse and, over the next several days, Tatti slipped in and out of consciousness. We almost lost him a couple of times. But finally, on January 1, he sat up in bed and boomed,

"Healthy soul in a healthy body... a hungry body! Is it the new year yet?"

Mame and I rushed to his side and Mame scolded,

"Oh, you old Malzonik" (that's "husband" in Polish)... "you will never learn to stay at home in a storm."

"If the old goat didn't jump, he'd have a miserable life!" Our Tatti was back.

Tatti's final entry, on New Year's Day, is a treasure I'll guard in my heart forever.

The doctor said my wife and son and dog kept vigil by my side that whole Christmas week. I just slept and dreamed and slept and dreamed. I guess that's when I saw Him. I saw Jesus. He was not the man in the stained glass windows of our church. He was not a tiny baby in a manger scene. He was not a Nazi or a Pole or a U.S. soldier. He was just... HIM... indescribable! He spoke. He said, "Josef... when you suffered, I suffered too." That was all He said. That was all I needed.

I heard the doctor say, "His condition is if-y." He was right...

If it hadn't been for a faithful sheltie,

If it hadn't been for my Ester's love,

If it hadn't been for my Jason's prayers... I might not be alive.

Oh, the "ifs." I do not understand them much at all. But I know now...

If not for Jesus, I would not know comfort. I would be stuck in misery. He unstuck me!

There now... that's more than enough words for a wise head!

Jason ran his hand across the precious note Tatti had inserted in his album. He blotted the tear that fell on the yellowed page. Then he looked lovingly to his children.

"I hope you were glad to hear a little more about your amazing legacy. Tatti not only survived that Christmas Day accident. He lived another 20 years. He passed away peacefully at age 83. Mame died later that same year and I know they are enjoying heaven together!"

"I still remember Tatti, Dad," Alex spoke up. "I think I was eight when he died. I'm sure glad he didn't die that Christmas. And I really liked learning more of his story tonight."

"I can remember him too," Caroline added. "He always seemed so happy!"

"Those extra years were a blessing because, once Tatti really met Jesus, he was an even more wonderful man than he had been before."

"I wish I would have known him," Jo pouted.

"Actually, you did meet him," his father added, "although you were only about one when he died. But he loved you very much. You're named after him, you know. 'Jo' is short for 'Josef' and that was Tatti's name."

"Then I want to be just like him," the youngest member of the clan exclaimed, "only... only I don't have a dog!"

The rest of the room burst out laughing and Jo's mom said it was time for hot chocolate refills. Disappearing from the room, she was back in a moment, not with a thermos of cocoa, but with a duffle bag, unzipped at the corner.

The Journal

"What's that Mom?" three eager children gathered round her.

Jason laid his father's precious album back on the coffee table by the nativity scene. Then he carefully took the bag from his wife and set it on the floor.

"Jo-Jo" (the old name slipped out). "Would you solve the mystery of the duffle bag please?"

Before Jo could even finish unzipping the top of the bag, a tiny black nose wiggled its way upward.

"A puppy!" Caroline squealed.

"I can't believe it." Alex seemed stunned. "Dad and Mom... you really got us a dog? I can't believe it!"

"Believe it. He's right here." The youngest family member cuddled the adorable pup. "And we all know his name, right?" Jo looked commandingly at his siblings.

"Bissel!" Alex and Caroline replied in joyful unison.

"I don't think so," Jo shook his head stubbornly at his siblings. He rubbed his face in the little dog's soft fur. "That's just not right. Tatti wouldn't call him that!"

Jo surveyed the family members and his eyes met his father's questioning look. Slowly a sly smile appeared.

"His name's not Bissel," he insisted. But then he laughed. "His name is... *Bissel Number Two!*"

But be doers of the word,
and not hearers only...

James 1:22 (NKJV)

Do not withhold good from
those to whom it is due,
when it is in your power to act.

Proverbs 3:27 (NKJV)

The Doers

"**O**kay everybody... this year it's my turn. All right?"

Seven pairs of eyes pivoted to the middle-aged woman who had just entered the living room, bearing a large tray of steaming mugs of hot chocolate. She set it down right next to the nativity scene, which occupied center-stage on the mammoth coffee table in the middle of the room. Lights twinkled on the fragrant pine in the corner. A few snowflakes drifted past the window.

It was Christmas Eve and Laura Sherman's family was settling in for their annual Christmas tradition... a story... typically told by the oldest member of the clan, Laura's father. The elderly gentleman chose a cup of cocoa and eased himself into the wing chair always reserved for him.

"Fine by me," the slender, silver-haired Alexander Petersohn nodded to his daughter.

"Me too." His namesake, 17-year-old Alex lifted his cup in agreement and took a spot on the floor, next to his gentle-natured 15-year-old sister, Caroline.

Jo, the youngest member of the clan, and undisputed clown of the family, considered himself, at 10, too big to occupy his normal perch on the arm of his grandpa's chair. Instead, he parked himself on the floor, leaning back against his grandfather's legs. He was so occupied blowing on his cocoa that he seemed oblivious to the topic being discussed.

"You know what, everybody?" Jo swished the contents in his mug. "Last night I dreamed we were all here together, and we were surrounded by an ocean of hot chocolate. Then suddenly it turned from brown to bubbly orange. That's when I woke up and discovered it was really only a *Fanta-sea!* Get it?"

A collective groan erupted from the rest. Jo had recently discovered puns and took advantage of any opportunity to impress his family with his comic prowess.

"Back to your mother's question... I tried my hand at story-telling last year," Jason Sherman, Laura's preacher husband laughed, "and considering you all have to listen to my sermons every week, I won't subject you to more of my ramblings."

"Yeah, but your 'ramblings' had one of the best endings ever!" Caroline reminded him as she patted the head of Bissel Number Two, the playful sheltie who had made his surprise arrival at the conclusion of the prior year's story... much to the entire family's delight.

Jo interrupted once again. "Yeah, Bissell made it a real Feliz Navi-*dog!*"

Another group moan.

"Very funny, Jo. But really, what about the rest of you? Would either of you like to have the floor this year?" Laura looked to Aunt Ingrid, her father's sister who, along with her 68-year-old parrot, Pilate, had recently come to live with them.

"Oh no. You all heard from me two years ago. I'm afraid I'm fresh out of stories."

"And don't look at me either," a second silver-haired gentleman piped up. "I'm just a guest of that old codger over there." Alberto Jiordano, the chunky-built, distinguished friend of the family's patriarch, smiled broadly and tilted his thumb towards his buddy. "No story from me. I've been really looking forward to sitting back and enjoying the evening with all of you."

Warm drink in hand, he lowered himself onto an old creaky rocker and winked merrily at his hostess.

"Go for it, my dear."

All eyes focused expectantly on Laura as she squeezed onto the sofa beside her husband.

"Hang on a second." It was Jo again. He jumped up and quickly turned off several lamps, transforming the room into a beautiful setting, illumined only by a few candles and the glow from the tree. "There, I thought I should do this because it would make you all *de-lighted!*"

Rolled eyes, shaking heads and chuckles from his tiny audience.

"Oh Jo-Jo," his mother exclaimed, "you are really something, you know that? Now, if you will please keep quiet for a bit, I would like to proceed with my story. It's about a boy called AJ who, like you my dear son, loved to joke around. I heard this tale several years ago. I've never forgotten it and figured you might all enjoy hearing it too, some Christmas Eve. So, I guess tonight's the night..."

AJ and his family lived in a small town in the 1950's. Like most of the families in that community, they were immigrants who had fled Europe due to the Second World War. The town, in fact, was a melting pot for a hodge-podge of nationalities and ethnic backgrounds.

Those were difficult years. Adults worked long and hard supporting their families, so the children were often left on their own for most of the day. AJ was a prankster and it didn't take him long to gather a gang of other young teens bent on mischief. He thrived on leading his crew into one escapade after another. One of his pals, a guy everyone called "Slim," was AJ's right-hand man and together the two made a formidable team.

AJ professed to be a Christian, so he knew he should not let his practical jokes get too out-of-hand. His troupe tended to confine their pranks to fairly-innocent stuff. They substituted sugar in saltshakers. They rotated all their households' furniture fifteen degrees just to confuse the family members. They attached bicycle horns under sofa cushions and toilet seats where they would sound when an unsuspecting person sat.

AJ particularly loved to plant things in his friends' shoes. He would cram one of his own sweaty socks in the toes, so the shoes wouldn't fit and, when the target of the prank removed the stuffing, they were almost overcome by the nasty odor.

One day, AJ's mother asked him to make a trip to the bank to deposit ten dollars in the family's account. When the boy arrived and approached the teller, he promptly bent over, untied his muddy sneaker and plunked it on the counter right in front of the poor woman. He reached in to remove the ten one-dollar bills he had stashed there. By the time he laid them, damp and wrinkled, in front of her, she was almost fainting. The boy's foot odor could be overpowering.

Another time, he and Slim filled a hot-water bottle with mashed-up leftover ravioli and canolis, then taped the bottle inside AJ's shirt. They went to school and innocently waited for the lunch bell to ring. At that precise moment, AJ doubled over, moaning loudly as though he wasn't feeling well. Forcefully clutching his stomach, he sent the gross-looking mixture spewing upwards like a fountain. As other students jumped back in disgust, Slim stepped forward with a fork, and began chowing down on the colorful mess.

Yes, AJ could be quite a rascal and it seemed he got his greatest joy tormenting others with his gags. Unfortunately, as time passed, he and his cohorts grew less content with simple tricks. They began moving on to bigger and more risky plots. When they planted a string of firecrackers in the furnace room of the church and actually caught the building on fire, people began to worry what might be next. But to AJ, it was all just a lot of harmless fun and he had no intention of stopping.

Until a widower and his daughter moved in next door...

Mr. Sargent was what today we might call "a hick." He was a British hillbilly-type with atrocious grammar and a thick Cockney accent. But he exuded such a friendly, chipper attitude, he was liked and respected by all he met. He lost no time settling into the community and quickly became a member at the local church... the same one AJ and most of his band of followers attended, at their parents' command.

The newcomer observed immediately that this gang of scamps was headed down a dangerous path. Though their jokes so far hadn't seriously hurt anyone, he could see they were escalating in that direction. The older man knew they needed to be set on a more productive course, so he volunteered to teach them during the Sunday School hour each week. The boys liked the man well enough but often whispered amongst themselves and paid little attention to his Bible lessons. His daily prayer was that somehow the Lord would break through their care-less attitude and capture their souls.

Mr. Sargent's teenage daughter Mariella was just as delightfully pleasant as her father, although her speech and demeanor were soft and refined. She was warm, witty, and pretty besides. From the first time AJ laid eyes on her, he was smitten. He determined to win her heart.

Of course, AJ knew only one way to get attention and that was through his tomfoolery. So he concocted a prank to gain Mariella's attention.

It seemed mild enough. He attached several plastic spiders to a thread. Then, when he knew Mariella was away from the house, he sneaked next door and taped the end of the thread to the top of the screen door so that the row of bugs would fall right in front of her when she opened the door. Then he hid in the bushes, awaiting her arrival. He anticipated she would scream, at which point he would make his heroic appearance to swat down the bugs and earn her admiration.

He didn't bargain on the fact that Mariella, though strong in faith and character, had one besetting fear: *spiders*. When the fake insects plummeted right before her nose, the poor young woman screamed all right... and then fainted dead away! Falling backwards, she cracked her head with a sickening thud on the concrete sidewalk and lay there unconscious.

Stricken with panic and remorse, AJ rushed to her side, yelling for Mr. Sargent. The two men picked up Mariella and carried her to the living room couch. Mr. Sargent got a cold cloth for her forehead while AJ fanned her frantically.

She lay there pale and dead to the world. Fortunately, after several minutes, the girl's eyes fluttered. She sat up shakily and, still terrified, informed her father that their house was being invaded by an army of black spiders. Mr. Sargent went to the front door and returned with the strand of culprits dangling from his hand.

"AJ, ya wouldna happ'n to know any'ing 'bout these 'ere *plas'ic* spiders, would ya now?"

To AJ's credit, he wasn't one to lie, so, greatly embarrassed, he confessed. Besides, he was tremendously sorry for the fright and near-serious injury he had caused. The whole incident had really shaken him.

It was just the moment Mr. Sargent had been waiting for. He knew that AJ was the ringleader of the town's young men. If AJ's heart could be harnessed for Christ, he figured many others would follow. He sat down beside the boy and picked up his Bible.

"AJ, Lis'en now t'ese 'ere verses. Da firs' is James 1:22... *be doers of da word, and na 'earers only, deceivin' yerselves.* Da sec'nd is Proverbs 3:27... *D'na wi'old good from those t'whom 'tis due, when 'tis in yer pow'r t'act.*"

"AJ, ya has Jesus in ya, but me thinks He na 'ave all yer 'eart. Ya wants fun 'n games 'n jokes and ya spends a bushel o'time dreamin' up yer schemes. But Jesus' schemes and dreams will do a sight more good, an' trus' me, in da long run, yer'll be a sight more 'appy!"

That was it... brief and to the point... and it hit home with AJ. After all, he had almost murdered the woman he loved. The young man went away deep in thought.

Over the next few days, he returned for further conversation with Mr. Sargent. In his simple way, the Godly man challenged AJ to begin looking for ways to use his endless energy for good... practical things he could do to show God's love and joy to folks in the town. He told AJ that, if he saw a need he could meet or a situation he could help with, he should jump in and "Git t' doin' it!"

So that was what AJ did. Over the next months, he began asking God to show him every day something he could do to make a difference. His one-man crusade soon spread to the other boys in the Sunday School class and they became a squad of home-town heroes, helping the elderly, teaching children, cleaning up public places, and generally bringing great joy to their families. They gave their group a name... The Doers. Not only did they gather on Sundays, they began meeting at Mr. Sargent's home during the week for Bible study and prayer. The group of troublesome boys gradually transformed into a powerful Christian influence in their little town and even in the surrounding region.

Much of what they did was not earth-shattering... just daily good deeds that demonstrated the kindness the Lord was cultivating in their hearts. There were, however, a couple of occasions when their quick action was life-saving.

One late summer day, word spread that a local toddler was lost. His parents had combed their neighborhood with no success. On a no-doubt-God-inspired hunch, AJ and The Doers decided to head to the edge of town in a completely different direction from the other searchers. They spread out across a nearby cornfield. Row by row they inched forward, praying all the time. It was Slim who spotted the little tike fast asleep, almost completely camouflaged among the stalks. That corn crop was scheduled to be chopped only a few hours later. The Doers had saved the little fellow's life.

What rejoicing and gratitude filled the townsfolks' hearts that day!

Another time, right in the middle of a sermon, a parishioner suddenly began wildly flailing his arms and pointing to his throat. While most of the congregation sat motionless, AJ jumped to his feet, hurdling three pews to reach the man's side. Several of The Doers followed close behind. AJ, by now a strapping 18-year-old, hoisted the man to his feet and then forcefully slung him over the back of the seat in front of him. With his buddies' help, AJ lifted him again and once more brought his ribs down hard on the wooden pew-back. It took a few additional tries but finally the man lurched forward, coughed, and with a strenuous gag, the hard candy that had blocked the poor man's windpipe went

flying clear up to the communion table. The pastor closed the service right then and there with a heart-felt prayer of praise.

AJ and The Doers didn't only help with crises like these. They became so excited about the truth of scripture and the reality of Jesus' presence in their own lives, they couldn't keep quiet about it. Their testimony was responsible for drawing many in that town to faith in Christ.

"Mom, did AJ quit being a funny guy?" It was Jo interjecting. "Did he stop doing jokes?"

"Yeah, I was wondering the same thing," his older brother agreed. "And no offense Mom, the story's been great but there really isn't much about *Christmas* in it."

"And whatever happened to Mariella?" Caroline continued. "And Mr. Sargent... did he let AJ marry his daughter?" She glanced at their guest who seemed to be studiously avoiding her eyes.

The storyteller grinned.

"I'm not finished yet," she stated with a mischievous grin. "Just hang on for the rest of the story of AJ... I don't think you will be disappointed."

AJ did not quit being a funny guy just because he became a zealous follower of the Lord. He still had a fantastic sense of humor, and there was rarely an interaction with AJ that didn't include lots of laughter.

And yes, he and Mariella became best friends. The spider incident was long forgotten and she learned to appreciate his unpredictable sense of humor. She never knew what he would do next.

When AJ was 19, he was ready to propose. He sought and received Mr. Sargent's whole-hearted blessing. By now, AJ had the firmly-established habit of getting right to it, once he decided to act. So he was not going to delay in asking Mariella to marry him.

He decided he would invite his sweetheart to dinner the following Saturday... the first weekend of December. There was only one fine restaurant in town, a tiny but elegant place. Neither of them had ever been there. Eating out was a very rare treat in those days. They

would enjoy dinner together at the fancy establishment and then AJ planned to pop the question and present her with a ring after dessert.

The special date arrived and AJ was a bundle of nerves. He dressed in his Sunday best. He slicked down every strand of his unruly mop with hair tonic. He had even found a pair of shiny new shoes at the local second-hand store and purchased them for the occasion. They were a little big for him so he stuffed the toes with two of his hankies to make them fit better. It was a frustrating process getting ready for such a big event. AJ was so keyed up he could hardly make his fingers button his shirt or knot his tie.

Nevertheless, he finally called on Mariella and they headed out into the wintery evening. AJ was more jittery than he had ever been in his life. He tripped over his own feet several times on their stroll to the restaurant. He clunked his head on the restaurant door as he opened it for Mariella, almost knocking himself out. When he attempted to seat her at the table, instead of pushing her chair forward, he pulled it backward and sent her sprawling on the floor. And he had to excuse himself from the table twice to go to the bathroom. His heart pounded. His hands were sweaty. His forehead broke out in drops of perspiration. He reached into his pocket, fingering the rolled-up handkerchief in which he had carefully hidden the tiny engagement ring, that had cost him much of his meager life-savings.

When they finally finished the last bite of dessert, AJ leaned across the table and took Mariella's hand.

"Mariella, I, uh... well, you know we, uh..." He just couldn't get the words out. "Oh... I don't know how to say it. So... *here!*"

Removing the soft cloth package from his pocket, he laid it dramatically in front of his sweetheart and waited expectantly for her to unroll the cotton fabric. His eyes fixed on her face, anticipating her delighted response.

Instead, Mariella looked at him with a quizzical frown.

"Ummm... AJ, why are you giving me this hanky?"

"Finish unrolling it, Mariella! See what's inside!" He urged.

She picked up a corner of the cloth and shook it over the table. Nothing!

Horrified, AJ grabbed it and shook it too. Where was the ring? He began frantically patting the tablecloth. He lifted their dessert dishes and felt underneath. He looked in their water tumblers. Then he was down on his hands and knees, crawling under the table, his head inches from the carpet. No ring. AJ was panic-stricken!

He ran his hands frantically back and forth on the rug. Where could the ring be? In his confused frenzy, he even reached for his beloved's foot, yanked off her shoe, turned it upside down and shook it. Nothing! Mariella seemed calmly amused by the whole affair. AJ was perspiring profusely.

As he was about to grab for her other shoe, a thought suddenly struck him. Of course! The young man crawled out from under the table and returned to his own seat. Reaching down, he yanked off his own shoe and plunked it ceremoniously on the table in front of Mariella.

"It's in there, my dear!" he announced. "Go ahead... I guess I just got the handkerchiefs mixed up."

Strong waves of stinky-feet smell were now wafting upwards and Mariella covered her nose with one hand. With the other, she reached reluctantly into the sweaty loafer and removed the wad of cloth. She unrolled it gingerly but once again found nothing.

By now, the foot-smell was reaching neighboring diners and, before long, others were covering their noses and pointing in the direction of the young couple. But AJ didn't notice. With a "Please, Lord, let it be in this one," he removed his other shoe and placed it with a dramatic thud next to the first.

"I'm sure it's in this one!" he assured Mariella.

And so it was. With one hand still shielding her nose, Mariella finally drew out the shiny ring and slid it on her finger. She waved her hand high for all in the restaurant to see. The customers applauded and cheered, while still trying to fan away the offending aroma.

It had not been a typical proposal. Nevertheless, the young couple was ecstatic.

The following week, AJ and Mariella were married in a simple service.

Mr. Sargent entrusted his daughter to AJ, admonishing him to look for things that would be a blessing to his wife and then, "just do 'em!" As an afterthought, he added, "An' do na' be playin' any o' yer jokes on 'er neither!"

The whole Doers class was present and gave the new husband and wife a rousing send-off.

"Just remember, you two agreed to be Mary and Joseph for the Christmas program," Slim called after them.

"We'll be there," the newlyweds assured them.

Sure enough, when Christmas Eve arrived, AJ and Mariella, aka Joseph and Mary, were in the basement Sunday school classroom, donning their costumes. The lovebirds were still practically walking on air. They looked forward to spending their lives serving the Lord together, and what better way to get started, they had reasoned, than to help out with the Christmas production.

Earlier that day, AJ visited a local farm and brought in several armfuls of straw to fill the manger for baby Jesus. The Son of God would actually just be a doll in a blanket, since the infant cast for the part had come down with croup just that morning. But that didn't really matter because the baby would be so low in the manger no one in the audience would be able to see Him anyway. The straw spilling over the side of the crude box would add a realistic touch.

Finally the service was about to begin. AJ and Mariella lined up with the rest of The Doers class who, to the pastor's relief, had cheerfully volunteered to fill all the other nativity roles. They were now a comical-looking bunch of angels, shepherds, wise men and barn animals.

As the procession entered the candle-lit sanctuary and began its walk down the center aisle, a hush fell over the congregation. The organ played "Silent Night" softly in the background. Joseph and Mary led the way, followed by the angels and shepherds, then the animals and finally the wise men. The young couple took their spot by the Holy Infant's crude bed. The shepherds and wise men knelt reverently around the manger.

It was their beloved Mr. Sargent who then rose and began reading the Christmas accounts from Luke 2 and Matthew 2. There was something refreshingly authentic hearing the familiar words through his Cockney accent.

As he closed the Bible, all eyes fixed worshipfully on the touching Christmas scene.

Mariella, herself a new bride, was feeling much of the same emotion Mary must have felt that star-lit night. She looked at AJ, love shining in her eyes. He smiled at her tenderly and then they both turned to gaze at the precious baby in the manger.

The pastor rose for the closing prayer and solemnly began, "Our dear heavenly Father, we…"

But he never finished because a blood-curdling scream suddenly erupted from center stage. Every eye jerked open, just in time to see the young mother collapse unconscious onto the arm of her husband. AJ, frantically surveying the situation, immediately saw the reason for his wife's ill-timed shriek. With a quick flourish, he reached down with his free hand and removed his shoe. Struggling valiantly to support his blacked-out wife with one arm, while managing his lethal weapon with the other, he began swatting at the Christ Child repeatedly. Whack! Whack! Whack!

A horrified gasp went up from the congregation.

AJ gave a final whack and then turned to the audience.

"Uh… sorry folks… it was a big one… a spider… my wife doesn't do very well with spiders… the baby's fine, though… look!"

He dropped the deadly loafer in the straw and, grabbing the doll's arm, swung the baby high, while still supporting his out-cold wife. It dangled upside down, head flopping. Another horrified gasp erupted, since most of the congregation hadn't been informed that a fake baby had replaced a live one.

"See… the baby's fine. It's not real, you know… I mean, Jesus is real, but this one isn't. And Mary will be okay in a minute or two. We've actually been through this before."

AJ glanced at Mr. Sargent who was scrambling to make his way to his daughter's side. The older gentleman eyed AJ suspiciously.

"It was crawling in the straw… I didn't put it there… well I guess maybe I did… but it wasn't one of my old tricks! I promise you… *Dad.*"

In a sudden burst of medical genius, AJ dropped the baby back in its crib, picked up his shoe and waved it in front of his wife. One whiff brought immediate results!

Mariella began blinking and shook her head, slowly regaining sensibility. With one hand covering her nose, she used her other hand to steady herself against her husband. Then she straightened up and reached for the poor infant in the insect-ridden bed. Tenderly she cradled the baby, brushing away a few clinging wisps of straw. Now, back in her Biblical role, she gazed at the doll, as lovingly as if it had been the Christ Child Himself.

A relieved Mr. Sargent grinned and looked back to the audience…

"D'na wi'old good from those t'whom 'tis due, when 'tis in yer pow'r t'act. Me 'as to think that Joseph did exac'ly that t'night. An' me thinks our Savior did exac'ly that when He saw we all be needin' savin'. He walloped da ol' en'my once n' fer all. He was a do-er and 'tis because o' Him, me and you kin git to be doers too!"

A collective sigh swept through the room, followed by a roar of laughter, as Joseph wrapped both arms around his wife in an uninhibited embrace and planted a huge kiss on Mary's cheek. AJ was a doer all right!

It was a Christmas not one of them would ever forget.

Laura Sherman surveyed the loved ones gathered around her.

"And I hope not one of you will forget it either."

"Well Mom, I have to admit that turned out to be a pretty good story." Alex lifted his now-empty cup in a mock salute. "But tell us, did this *really* happen? Was there a real AJ?"

"I believe it's a true story," Caroline interrupted. "And I'm pretty sure I know who the main character really is!" she announced triumphantly. She pointed her finger accusingly at their grandpa's guest, who had a sly smile on his face.

"You're AJ, aren't you, Mr. Jiordano? Mr. *Alberto Jiordano?*"

The elderly Italian's smile broadened. He tipped his chin as though beginning a nod, but then he shook his head.

"You're on the right track, Caroline, but no, I am not AJ. I'm..." He paused. "I'm the pasta-chowing *Slim.*"

"What?" the three children chorused. "Then who...?"

Their mother rose and stepped to her father's side.

"Allow me to introduce you to ornery, fun-loving AJ... Alexander *Jakob* Petersohn, otherwise known as your grandfather."

The old gentleman's eyes twinkled.

"That was a very long time ago, after my family moved west from New York." He patted his daughter's arm. "Your mother told you all that stuff about me, didn't she?"

"Yes, not long before she died, she told me the whole story." Laura grinned at her father, "And lots more, actually."

Alexander Petersohn, a far-away look on his face, sighed deeply.

"You know, Slim and I aren't really the heroes of that story. If it weren't for Mr. Sargent, our lives would have been very different. And if it weren't for my sweet, sweet Mariella..." his voice choked.

His sister interjected.

"Mariella was the cheeriest, kindest, most giving person I ever met. I thanked God often for blessing me with such a wonderful sister-in-law. You children would have loved her. Everyone who knew her loved her."

The elderly patriarch, now composed, bent forward as though about to reach for his shoe. Jo instinctively scooted away and put his hand over his nose.

"Oh, don't worry, Jo. I don't hide things in my shoes anymore... too far to bend. Although I can assure you my wife took care of my stinky feet problem years ago."

He reached instead into his jacket pocket and removed a neatly-folded white handkerchief. Rising stiffly, he shufffled towards the coffee table. Laying the little fabric package in front of the nativity, he folded back the top flap and withdrew a small gold ring.

"This was your grandmother's ring." He held it up. In the tree-light, it sparkled. "On the inside, is engraved James 1:22, 'Be doers of the word.' That is also engraved on the inside of my ring. We took that as our life verse."

He laid it right next to the carved baby Jesus in the manger.

"I think we all need to remember that we can only be doers, I mean doers who make a real, lasting difference, because He was one first. That is the great message of Christmas... what Jesus did by coming into the world and giving His life for all of us sinners who desperately needed saving."

Then, with an unexpected chuckle, AJ unfolded the second flap of the handkerchief and drew out another small object, concealing it mysteriously in his palm.

"I've kept this in the top drawer of my bureau, as a constant reminder that every day I have a choice whether to do things to help or hurt. Of course, I always made sure it was hidden from Mariella."

With a flourish, he dropped a realistic-looking black plastic spider right next to the manger.

"Come to think of it, there probably were some live bugs in baby Jesus' bed. I wonder if Joseph did anything about them."

I hope for Mary's sake, he did," the evening's story-teller laughed. "Ugh! I think I must have inherited my mother's dislike for spiders." Then, surveying the group, Laura added,

"But I want you all to know my earnest Christmas prayer is that all of us will be life-long doers too, just like AJ and Mariella and Slim and all the rest... but, please... *without* the spiders!"

At which point, Jo, always eager to have the last word, jumped to his feet.

Seven sets of eyes fixed curiously on the youngest member of the clan.

"Just think, you met Grandma and fell in love. You decided to... *marry... merry... Mariella.* And 'cause of that, we are here drinking hot chocolate on Christmas Eve. Yes, Siree... " He swept his arm around the picture-postcard setting.

"Just think, everybody, our whole merry Christmas is on account of..."

He pointed accusingly at his grandfather, then the fake spider, then back again at his grandpa. And with a wit worthy of AJ himself, Jo Petersohn pronounced,

"It's all on account of... you... *spied-her!*"

Author's Postscript

The characters and events in this story are fictitious, with one exception. There was a real-life Mr. Sargent who took it upon himself to do something for the souls of a bunch of boys, mostly immigrants in the city where I grew up, in Canada. He began teaching the Bible to them, and it wasn't long until they caught their mentor's zeal for service and named themselves, "The Doers." From that class of over 40 young men, came pastors, missionaries, lay preachers, and a whole troop of committed Christians that entered all walks of life and shared their faith far beyond their home town.

My father was one of those young men influenced for eternity by a humble, unsophisticated man who, according to Dad, "murdered the King's English." Which just goes to show, I suppose, that when we give our lives to Christ, it is truly amazing what He can do through us! Not just at this Christmas time... but for many, many years yet to come.

In his defense Jesus said to them,
"My Father is always at his work
to this very day,
and I too am working."

John 5:17

Through the Oven Glass

"It's just a lot of work. Hard, hard work. Christmas isn't supposed to be like this!" Katie fumed. "That's all it is... just plain...hard... work!" Each word was punctuated with a jab by her rubber-gloved hand. Katie was on her knees, in a most unflattering position, fiercely scrubbing the inside of her old oven.

"Why couldn't I have a self-cleaning oven?" the young mother complained to herself. "After all, it's the 70's... all my friends have self-cleaning ovens... why not me?" she gave another stab at a particularly-stubborn spot. "Of course I know why. That cheap husband of mine thinks he has to have every new gadget under the sun for his office, but would he ever think of buying me a new stove? Fat chance!"

Actually, Katie dearly loved Ben. Most of the time, she considered him a wonderful mate but, at this particular moment, she wanted to blame somebody for her predicament. Her husband was a convenient somebody.

She pushed a strand of hair upward, off her nose and swiped her palm across her sweaty forehead. Then she sat back wearily on the newspaper-covered kitchen tile. It was spattered with wet brown drips from her

scrub brush but Katie didn't care. Her aching back and sore arms needed a breather. She leaned against a table leg and thought back on the events that had led up to this morning... Christmas morning... with her on the floor in a grimy bathrobe, up to her elbows in grease and soot and, with every breath, inhaling those noxious oven cleaner fumes.

"What a miserable lot of work Christmas is!" Katie concluded once again.

Her oven problems had started weeks ago. Katie had been asked, as she was each year, to bring pies to her in-laws' Christmas get-together. They always celebrated early in December which was just fine with her since the rest of the month filled up so quickly with a slew of activities. Katie loved to bake and especially prided herself on her apple pies. Her children, Andy, Aaron, and Allison, told her every year that her pie was better than any apple pie in the whole world... the best they'd ever tasted. She never really believed them since she made her pies the same way each year. So it was unlikely that one year was noticeably superior to the prior. Besides, how many apple pies had her eight-, seven-, and four-year-old sampled? They were certainly

not the most experienced judges. She enjoyed their flattery, nevertheless.

Again this year she made her pies with care but packed a few more apples than usual into the perfectly-rolled crust. She wanted the pies to be exceptionally juicy and delicious. However, maybe those extra apples were not such a good idea. For the first time ever, the sweet contents of her pies bubbled up and over the sides of the pans onto the oven floor. Katie came running into the kitchen when she smelled something awful. Too late! Burned sugar and charred apples covered the bottom of the oven. Yuck!

Not only did it require two back-breaking hours to clean the old appliance, but Katie had to endure the humiliation of bringing *bought* pies to the family dinner! To make matters even worse, she made the mistake of feeding what remained of her ruined pies to their York-shire terrier puppy, Samson. He gladly devoured them and was thereby rewarded with three days of projectile diarrhea. This just *exploded* Katie's work load.

"And do you think Ben or the children would help me?" she continued in her mental gripe session. "No-o-o, Mom's supposed to do *everything!*"

Christmas Tales that warm the heart

The pie catastrophe was just the first of Katie's oven ordeals, however. As she sat fuming, she mentally relived episode number two...

Ten more December days had rushed by in a blur of busy-ness. Hours of effort went into preparations for Christmas programs. Each evening, Katie helped the children rehearse their parts for the school plays and the church pageant. She had to sew *three* costumes this year and, of course, they all required intricate work. Why couldn't her children have been assigned shepherd roles? She could have just wrapped up Andy, Aaron, and Allison in three old bathrobes and tied towels on their heads.

But no, Katie was stuck making a wise man's royal robes, plus donkey and sheep costumes. Not a simple assignment. She spent three consecutive nights working at her sewing machine until after midnight. While the rest of the family was nestled *all snug in their beds*, she wrestled with acrylic pile, sateen, breaking needles and threads.

Then Andy volunteered to bring plum pudding with caramel sauce to his school's Christmas party. He assured his mother that he would make it all by himself. Since the only parenting book Katie had ever read urged dads and moms to teach their children responsibility by letting them do things for themselves, Katie was thrilled to let Andy tackle the pudding project. She found recipes in a couple of her mother's old cookbooks and turned the kitchen over to her eight-year-old. *Big mistake!*

The pudding actually went pretty well with Andy managing to turn out a great specimen of the traditional dessert. It was the *stupid* sauce that caused the problem. While Andy was stirring the thick caramel-ly mixture, his father had arrived home with a freshly-cut Christmas tree. Ben called for the children to help him carry it into the living room of their old farmhouse. Naturally, Andy was excited to help and became totally engrossed in assisting his dad to position the tree straight and steady in the stand. It wasn't until Dad and children were all finished and proudly admiring the towering pine that Katie had come flying down the stairs, past them all, yelling,

"What's that smell? Can't the rest of you smell something burning? Andy, what are you doing in here? You're supposed to be stirring the sauce!"

They all had rushed into the kitchen to discover that the sauce had not only boiled over, covering the burner and most of the stovetop, but it had dripped through the burner hole and clear down into the hot oven. There it landed on the meatloaf Katie was baking for supper. Now she had a dirty oven and a ruined supper besides! Andy tearfully apologized and Ben even offered to help, but Katie, in angry exasperation, had ordered everyone out of the kitchen. As she feverishly scrubbed the second oven mess, she had concluded, indignantly, that the author of that parenting book obviously had never dealt with burned caramel sauce. Otherwise he would have urged the teaching of responsibility anywhere but in the kitchen.

"And now this... a third mess... and on Christmas morning!" Katie grumbled to herself. "Well, I can't just sit around here on the floor, or I'll never have the oven ready to use for our turkey dinner." Katie got back on her hands and knees and once again leaned her head and shoulders into that dark cavern. She scrubbed hard for several minutes, then rinsed her scouring brush in the bucket of brown water. She wiped her grimy hand across her forehead and attacked the remaining burned-on food.

"Shopping, gift wrapping, cookie baking, more shopping, going to all those pageants and programs, cleaning the house, decorating the house, sending out Christmas cards... and all of this on top of everything else I do as wife and mother around here! How's one person supposed to fit all that into one month?" Katie grumbled to herself.

Mentally, she did a fast rewind to the events that had led to this most-recent Christmas disaster...

Christmas Eve had arrived finally, and all the day's activities progressed smoothly. Katie had relaxed, believing her ordeals were in the past and that Christmas would actually turn out to be merry. After she got the children all tucked into bed, Katie had prepared her mother's famous scalloped potato recipe, filling a large glass casserole dish with the cheesy mixture. She put it in the oven, setting the timer for a delayed start. Since the oven was small, she planned to bake the potato dish in the early morning hours, then remove it and keep it warm on top of the stove while the turkey roasted. She knew she couldn't fit both turkey and potatoes in the oven at the same time. Katie went to bed at midnight, setting the alarm for five a.m.

Did she fail to set the start time correctly? Did she put in the wrong temperature? Katie never would figure out what went wrong. But when she awoke at five, it was to a suspiciously-familiar and ominous odor wafting up from the first floor. She threw on her bathrobe and, not even taking time for slippers, tore down the steps, through the living room to the kitchen. Black smoke was seeping through the oven door cracks! Instinctively, Katie grabbed a potholder and opened the door. It was

horrible… *horrible!* Somehow… she couldn't imagine how… the dish cradling her lovingly-prepared potatoes had cracked in two pieces. There were burned scalloped potatoes all over the racks and an inch deep on the oven floor.

"What in the world? Glass casserole dishes aren't supposed to break!" Katie screamed in her head. "Who made this pan? I'm going to sue that company!"

So that's how the young woman had ended up on her knees, cleaning the oven *again!*

"At least I'm finally done," she sighed as she wiped up the last of the potato ash. The oven was shining inside and out. She dropped the brush into her rinse bucket and sat back on the newspaper once more. She was tired. And she was disgusted with Christmas and all the work it entailed.

Suddenly she heard a thunderous sound, like a herd of stampeding elephants. Her husband, children, and puppy were charging down the steps and, in a moment, with great exuberance, they burst into the kitchen laughing and shouting, "Merry Christmas, Mom!"

Samson, upon seeing the newspaper all over the floor, ran straight to it to pee but, in his puppy clumsiness, skidded into the mop Katie had propped against the counter. The mop handle hit the roasting pan lid, which slid off the counter, ricocheting off the oven door handle, catching the rinse bucket at just the right angle to overturn it, spilling all the nasty contents! In the blink of an eye, Katie found herself sitting in a puddle... a gross, greasy puddle that covered most of the kitchen floor!

The exhausted wife and mother felt like crying, but was simply too stunned. She just sat there, the dirty water soaking through her bathrobe and PJ's.

The rest of the family stopped dead in their tracks. They stared in shocked silence at the mess and then at Katie who looked so forlorn and miserable. It was Ben who finally spoke. "Oh, Honey, look at you!" he said simply. He grinned warmly at his wife.

"So you think this is funny?" Katie snapped. "Like you all care that this Christmas has just been work, work and more work for me!"

"Mommy... you *should* look at you," four year-old Allison urged. "Is that *chocolate?*" she asked wide-eyed and pointed her finger at her mother's head.

"Of course it's not chocolate," Aaron replied.

"But Mom, you really should look at yourself!" Andy tapped his forehead.

"What on earth are you all staring at? Oh well, what the ...!" Almost she swore, but caught herself. Now drenched with greasy water, Katie got on her knees once more and leaned toward the oven window. She peered at her reflection in the now-gleaming glass. It was then that she saw what they were all seeing. Running from the tip of her nose to her hairline, and from one temple to the other across her forehead, Katie had unknowingly drawn a grimy, sooty cross!

In a flash, a parade of Christmas characters filled her mind: Joseph, packing up supplies for a rugged trip to Bethlehem... the shepherds, rounding up their stubborn, smelly sheep... the wise men, struggling with their camel loads... and Mary laboring to give birth in a stinky, filthy stable.

"I never really thought about it," Katie reflected. "Even the first Christmas must have required a lot of work. *Dirty* work, in fact!"

Ben squatted beside her and gently traced the ash-y outline of the cross on his wife's face. "You know, just like your work for all of us, Jesus' work was also a true labor of love."

In her mind, Katie pictured Jesus... exhausted, battered, and abandoned, struggling with the load of the cross, falling under its weight. He had worked with a purpose... the salvation of mankind, the salvation of Katie. She rested her head on her husband's shoulder.

"And our Savior kept at it 'til His work on earth was finished and that couldn't have been easy!" She chuckled, jumping to her feet and drawing her dripping bathrobe around her. A much happier wife and mother beamed at her family.

"You know what I'm thinking?" she asked with an air of exultation. "I'm thinking that Christmas *is* a lot of work. But I'm also thinking," and she shook her finger playfully at them all, "that a little hard work *never hurt anyone!* So, give me a hand everybody. Let's clean up this mess. Then we'll have a wonderful Christmas day celebrating our Savior who *never quits working.* In fact," she continued with enthusiasm, "it occurs to me that while I've been cleaning the oven, for the *third* time this month, God has been working that whole time too. After all, He has to get heaven ready for us. I guess that's giving Him lots to do. I imagine He's busy right now preparing the greatest Christmas feast ever!"

Katie bent down and started to gather up the soaked newspaper, stuffing it into the greasy rinse bucket. Then quietly, under her breath, she added with a grin, "I just pray for Jesus' sake that His pans aren't glass but, if they are, I sure do hope His ovens are *self-cleaning!*"

*This same Jesus,
who was taken up from you
into heaven,
will so come in like manner
as you saw Him go into heaven.*

Acts 1:11 (NKJV)

Just
Wait

Nate knew it was going to be a miserable Christmas… even worse than Thanksgiving had been. He was trying his best to be strong, but a huge ache had parked inside his 11-year-old chest. Since October, when his chaplain father left for an Air Force assignment in the Middle East, Nate had tried to be brave for his mother's sake. He knew she missed Dad too, although she obviously worked hard at being cheerful. But many nights, through her closed bedroom door, Nate heard her sniffling and during the day he often saw her eyes fill with tears. She was quick to wipe them away and force a smile but Nate could tell her emotion was as close to spilling out as his was. The baby of the family, 18-month-old Amy Sue, seemed blissfully unaware that her father was gone, except at mealtimes when she would point to his empty chair and say "Da-Da, Da-Da." At which point, his mom's eyes would once again get teary.

Somehow the three of them had made it through the turkey holiday, but Nate hadn't been very *thanks*-giving. In spite of hearing, "Don't worry. Just wait. He'll come back," at least a million times from aunts, uncles, cousins, and friends, his father's absence sucked the joy out of each day.

Now it was almost Christmas and every passing day was one more reminder of how merry-less the holiday would be.

The last school day before the holiday break arrived. All his classmates were so excited about their upcoming vacation. But Nate dreaded the very thought of Christmas break. He filed into the auditorium along with the other students, for the Christmas assembly. The room buzzed with typical pre-vacation anticipation. There were skits and songs and special presentations by each grade.

The curtain finally closed and the principal stepped forward for the usual, "Merry Christmas, Happy New Year" remarks. Then he paused and said, "Oh yes. Just one more thing... a special gift arrived today for two of our students..."

The stage curtains re-opened and there, in the middle of the stage, was a huge, brightly-wrapped box. The room fell silent when suddenly the package burst open and an Air Force Captain, handsome in his blue uniform and with a Santa Claus cap on his head, emerged, grinning. A third-grade boy and fourth-grade girl screamed "Daddy!" and flew down the aisle and up the steps to the waiting arms of their father. The room erupted in laughter, applause, whistles and screams as the rest of the students joined in the celebration. Nate smiled and clapped his hands too, but he looked at the scene through blurred eyes and his ache pounded even more painfully inside him.

He knew there would be no such surprise home-coming celebration for him. After all, his father had just left and one of the reasons for his deployment was so he could give spiritual and emotional support to the troops over Christmas.

Nate packed up his belongings and boarded the school bus with a heavy heart. While others laughed and carried on, he sat silent. Then, when the bus had almost arrived at his stop, he felt a poke in the back of his head. He knew it was Jeffrey, the new boy in his class, who had quickly established himself as the mean-est. In the relatively short time he had been attending their school, many kids had been the brunt of Jeffrey's bullying. Nate had learned quickly that not paying at-tention to Jeffrey was about the best way to get him to stop his pestering.

"Hey, Preacher's Kid," Jeffrey began. "Bet'cha wish that was your father in the big box today... huh?" Nate kept his gaze looking forward. Jeffrey continued, "But there's no way he'll come home for Christmas when he just left, right?" Then he laughed his typical mocking

laugh, "Unless, of course, they bring him home to you in a *pine* box! Get it?"

Nate steeled himself. But Jeffrey's cruel attack continued...

"Yeah. Just wait. He'll come, but he'll be *dead.*"

Nate wanted to whirl around and punch Jeffrey in the nose. But he couldn't give him the satisfaction of seeing the tears that had overflowed onto his cheeks. Thankfully, the bus pulled up in front of his home and, without a backward glance, he ran to the house, finally free from Jeffrey's taunting but not free from his worst fear.

Nate knew that his father was in danger. He had told Nate before leaving that there was the possibility he could be killed. It was 1990. Wars had been going on in that volatile and unpredictable area of the world for decades. But he had reassured Nate over and over, that he would do everything in his power to come back safe and sound to the family. They had prayed together and Nate tried to have faith that God would protect his dad.

"Just wait, he will come back!" he told himself re-peatedly. Nevertheless, Jeffrey's cruel words had planted a terror inside. A dark cloud of impending doom settled into his mind and he felt sick. Nate hid in his bedroom the rest of the day and tossed restlessly all night. Even in his dreams, he heard Jeffrey's mocking laughter.

When morning finally came, Nate determined to be strong for his mom and little sister. After all, it was Christmas Eve. However, the prospect of holidays without Dad made Nate feel miserable. Normally, winter vacations would be great times. Nate and his dad loved to build things together out in the workshop behind their house. Last year, they had put together a spectacular model airplane. There would be no one to work alongside this December. The weight of fear and sadness seemed twice as heavy as it had the day before.

He helped decorate a few cookies and then entertained his little sister so his mom could finish some food prep for the next day. Nate didn't know why she even put effort into fixing anything special for Christmas, when they both knew it would not be special at all without Dad.

Six-thirty came and the family of three donned winter jackets, climbed into their SUV and headed to Mount Olivet. This was a family tradition. For as long as Nate could remember, his family had joined other families from their church to present a short Christmas program for the residents of this nursing home. Folks from the surrounding community were invited as well and it always proved to be a fun evening. Nate had enjoyed it in the past. He could always hear his father's strong baritone voice "decking the halls," above everyone else. But his father's voice would not be heard this year... not on Christmas Eve and not on Christmas Day either.

His dad's voice was always the first sound he would hear on Christmas morning. It would come booming up from the first floor of the house, "Glory, Glory, Glory! It's Christmas. Jesus is born! Wake up everybody. Let's celebrate!" Nate would jump out of bed and fly down the stairs to be greeted with a big hug from his mom and a *high five* (now that he was almost a teenager) from his Dad. His family never gave a lot of gifts, but he could count on finding one gift for him and one for his sister, unwrapped, awaiting them under the Christmas tree.

He had received some nice presents through the years, but the highlight of Christmas for Nate had always been the fun traditions with his family. Without Dad's laughter and cheerfulness, without the enjoyment of working together on some new project, it just wouldn't be much fun. And what if his dad was never around for another Christmas?

Nate shook himself from his morbid thoughts. They had arrived at Mount Olivet and hurried into the large, brightly-lit, festively-decorated hall. Nate, and his mother carrying Amy Sue, found seats along with many other families.

This year was going to be different. Instead of the church families providing the entertainment for the seniors and community guests, the elderly residents had decided they wanted to present the program themselves. As Nate glanced at the residents seated in the front row, he recognized many of them. His dad had often led services at this facility and always hauled the whole family with him. Nate knew many of the old folks by name. Most of them were pretty frail. He couldn't imagine what they would do for a Christmas program.

"I'm sure they won't be dancing," Nate thought to himself, "they'd fall and not be able to get up." In spite of his gloomy mood, he couldn't help but grin at the thought.

The program was about to begin when Nate noticed a shabbily-dressed woman, followed by a just-as-shabbily-dressed boy take seats one row in front and across the aisle.

"Oh no," Nate moaned inwardly. "It's Jeffrey!" How could he enjoy the program with that kid as a constant distraction? Nate stared at the mother-son duo. He had never had much of a chance to really study Jeffrey, since the boy sat behind him on the bus and in class. He tried to interact with him as little as possible at school.

"I wonder where his father is," Nate mused. "Maybe he's dead, like he wishes mine was."

Suddenly Nate had a new thought... "Could Jeffrey's meanness have something to do with an absent father in his own life?"

Just then someone flashed the lights twice and a gentleman with a rather cockeyed white toupee stepped forward. He gave an enthusiastic welcome and led the audience in a couple of Christmas carols. Mrs. Jenkins played the old Hammond organ. She had three false starts on the introduction but, once she got going, she really made that instrument ring out and overall the singing sounded pretty good, even if it was missing his dad's baritone.

The emcee returned to the podium and read the Christmas story from Luke 2 and Matthew 2. Nate pretty much knew these passages by heart, since his father always read them on Christmas morning. Nate's eyes began to feel moist. He glanced at his mom and saw that she was blinking a lot.

"Why in the world did we even come?" he wondered. "This is just making Christmas even harder for us."

But then began the part of the program the residents had specially prepared for their guests. One by one, a resident came forward to give a little talk. Each represented a character from the Christmas account.

Nate smiled (in fact some of the audience chuckled out loud), as plump little Mrs. McMurray shuffled forward in her pink-flowered bathrobe. For a head-covering, she had a blue pad (the kind Nate had always seen on hospital beds) over her head. Leaning on her cane, she began,

"Good evening folks. I am Mary. Let me tell you a little about my life." She proceeded to recount her upbringing in Nazareth, her courtship and engagement to Joseph, her visit from the angel Gabriel, her hasty marriage and amazing trip to Bethlehem, her questions and concerns as her son grew, and the pain and agony of witnessing his execution. Nate had to admit she did a pretty good job and found himself wondering what the real Mary would have looked like as an old lady.

Following Mary was Mr. Stephens, aka Joseph. Also in a bathrobe and with a Mount Olivet-monogrammed towel tied around his head, he steadied himself with his two hands on his cane. He began his story. He shared about his life as a carpenter, the turmoil he experienced when he learned his fiancé was pregnant, the vivid dream encouraging him to go ahead and get married, the grueling and downright scary trip to Bethlehem and the astounding events surrounding Jesus' birth.

Mrs. Parker came forward pushing her walker and introduced herself as the prophetess, Anna. Somehow it was difficult to imagine the Bible character with a walker, loaded with Kleenex, her glasses case, and an assortment of books and magazines. When she let go of the walker to cross her arms as though cradling a baby, she almost lost her balance and a worried gasp went up through the audience, but she assured us she was fine and went on with her account.

The wise men were played by three elderly gentlemen in wheelchairs. Each chair was covered with a fuzzy brown flannel sheet and, between each elderly man's legs, he held a cardboard cut-out of a camel's head and hump. Again laughter rippled through the crowd as these men, atop their ships of the desert, reminisced. They told about their surprising astronomical discovery, their journey to Bethlehem "without a map or GPS," their audience with Herod whom they instinctively felt could not be trusted, the meeting with the holy family, and their warning dream and narrow escape from the evil monarch.

It was the most interesting perspective on Christmas that Nate had ever heard. These were real people, telling about real lives. The story of the Nativity had always been just that... a story. Tonight it came alive. He looked over at Jeffrey and his mother. They both appeared to be intently watching and listening. Jeffrey actually looked a little less mean.

But the seniors had saved their best for last. Nate recognized the man immediately as he strode to the microphone. Silver-haired and only slightly stooped, the man carried himself with confidence and dignity. He was dressed in a for-real shepherd's costume, complete with a sling-shot and staff. It was "General Nathaniel-Sir." At least, that's how Nate's dad had insisted his son always address the elderly veteran. He was a former Air Force General and, in the past whenever Nate accompanied his dad to the nursing home, they always ended up in fascinating conversations with General Nathaniel-Sir. Nate loved the man, partly because they shared the same name, partly because he was a military man like his father, but mostly because, aside from his dad, General Nathaniel-Sir was the most interesting person he had ever met.

"Good evening, everyone!" he began. "I was one of the shepherds on the Judean hillside, just outside the town of Bethlehem, the night Jesus was born. I was a boy of 11 at the time. My father, also a shepherd, insisted I was man enough to work with him in the fields. Shepherds were a rough and tough bunch of men and I wished there would have been at least one other boy among our crew. I desperately wanted a friend. It was a hard and lonely life. Day after day out in the wind and rain... little shelter really, never knowing if a wild animal or thief would be lurking somewhere in the shadows. And it was a difficult time in our Jewish his-

tory. The Romans had taken control of our nation and many Jewish families, including ours, were struggling just to survive. When my mother or I would complain about why Yahweh hadn't rescued us from such dire circumstances, my father always told us, 'Yahweh has promised to send a Rescuer, a Messiah, who will deliver us from our bondage. We must be patient and have faith and persevere. Just you wait,' he would tell us with firmness, 'He will come.'

"I'll never forget that night." The convincing-looking shepherd got a faraway look in his eyes. "I was stretched out on the ground, beside my father. Other shepherds were stationed strategically across the hillside, so as to be able to quickly sound an alarm should something or someone threaten the sheep. It had been a quiet night, until gradually there began a rustling amongst the sheep. They got restless like that when startled or when in danger. My father and I instantly sat up. I was excited. Perhaps I would get to try out my slingshot skills on a bear or a lion.

"We scanned the horizon along with the other shepherds who, at that point, were also awake and alert. At first we saw nothing. But then we spotted a man, a stranger, standing on one of the high boulders in the midst of the sheep. Though dark outside, as we pointed and stared, his image became clearer, almost like a spotlight was focused on him. But this was the middle of the night. Was he friend or foe? My dad motioned me closer and put his finger to his lips, warning me to remain quiet. I wondered if his heart was pounding like mine.

"And then the stranger spoke. Of course, you all know what he said. He told us not to be afraid because he had good news for us. He announced a Savior's birth in Bethlehem. He no sooner got those words out of his mouth than a whole crowd of dazzling figures surrounded him. The scene had become so bright, I had to shield my eyes, but I heard them clearly, 'Glory to God in the highest and on earth peace, good will toward men.'

"Well, when the shining beings disappeared, we shepherds decided to check out the stranger's words. We hurried to Bethlehem and, just as we had been told, we found a young couple, Joseph and Mary, with a new-born baby, in a cave behind the village inn. The parents said their child's name was Jesus. I felt so drawn to that baby. I had a deep desire to get to know him as he grew up. Perhaps we could even become friends.

"It was an amazing night and I was convinced that my father's promise was coming true. Certainly this baby would be the solution to our Jewish plight. Of course, he would have to grow up first.

"Weeks, months, a year went by. During that year, as often as I could get a break from my responsibilities,

I would hurry into Bethlehem and visit Joseph and Mary and Jesus. I had no siblings, so Jesus was fast becoming like my own baby brother. I envisioned us playing together for years to come. Then one day, when I went to his house, I found it empty. I asked around and, through townspeople, I learned that Jesus' family had moved away... left in a huge hurry. Some believed they had headed south towards Egypt. Others said they were Galileans, so surely they had headed north. My life as a shepherd kept me pretty much tied to the hills around Bethlehem, but I so badly wanted to know what became of that boy. Of course we had no newspapers, television, cell phones or internet, so to me it was as though he had dropped off the planet.

"Years went by. I grew up. I passed my 20th birthday, then my 30th. I got married and had my own family and, like my father, continued raising sheep. But I never forgot that strange night or that fun little boy.

"Finally, when I was in my 40's I heard a visiting rabbi talk about a man who was doing miracles and impressing many folks with his teaching. He said the man had grown up in Nazareth, but then moved to Capernaum and now travelled around teaching in synagogues and to large crowds in the countryside. He had developed quite a following and some hoped he might be the promised Messiah. When the rabbi said the man's name was Jesus, I was elated. I decided I must find him. I needed to find out if he was, in fact, the baby I'd known. I needed to discover if our Messiah had indeed come.

"I left my own boys in charge of our sheep and spent much of the next couple of years travelling from town to town, asking for information about Jesus. It seemed that I was always just a couple of steps behind Him. In every town, I'd ask about Him.

"'Oh yes, He was here just last month, but He moved on now. Perhaps you'll find Him in...' and then they would name yet another town. On I'd go.

"Soon after my 44th birthday, I became deeply discouraged. If Jesus was the Messiah, it seemed to me that by now He should have taken the country by storm. Yet all I heard were reports of good teaching and heal- ings which, although that sounded interesting, gave no hint of military action whatsoever. I could never forget the events of that night so long ago, but I felt perhaps it was time to give up on the idea of Jesus being anyone very special.

"The Passover holiday came and, as always, I cel- ebrated with my family but only half-heartedly. Passover was as important to our families as Christmas is to you today. I remembered how my father would say, 'Just wait. He'll come!' with such certainty. Well, I recited those words to my own family as part of our religious

tradition, but with no conviction at all. Jesus had come... that much I knew... but as for rescuing anyone, apparently that was never to happen.

"A few weeks went by and some visitors arrived in town. They told an incredible story and it spread like wildfire through Bethlehem. They said they had come from Jerusalem where they celebrated the Passover. A man, Jesus, who had been thought to be the Jews' promised Messiah, had been executed, crucified actually. 'But,' they said, 'the amazing thing is, in the past month there are reports that He has been seen alive!'

"Once again, my heart stirred with a desire to look for Jesus. Perhaps there was yet hope of finding him. So I took off for Jerusalem. It was only about six miles from Bethlehem. I could be there in a few hours. The events surrounding the birth of the baby Jesus had been hard to believe so it occurred to me that events surrounding His death might also be supernatural. I had to try to find out if this Jesus was the baby boy I'd known.

"As I headed north towards Jerusalem, I had a strong sense that I should detour toward the village of Bethany, east of the capital. I had visited Bethany once before on one of my searches. Reports were that Jesus had friends there. *Friends*... I had once hoped He would be my friend. But I had never caught up with Him. Of course He would have made other friends. There had even been accounts of Him raising one of His pals from the dead.

"As I approached Bethany, on a hillside just outside of town, I spotted a group of people huddled together. They were pointing to the sky. A huge cloud hovered overhead. I started to run towards them. Memories of the night outside Bethlehem replayed in my mind. We shepherds had gathered and pointed too. I tried not to stumble over the rocky terrain, as I kept my eyes on those men up ahead. Suddenly, I stopped dead in my tracks. I stared. Fading into that enormous cloud was the form of a man. I rubbed my eyes and blinked. As quickly as I had seen Him, He disappeared from sight. I thought I must have imagined it, but no, the crowd was still pointing and looking up.

"As I watched the huddled group, trying to decide whether I should approach them and ask what was going on, two men dressed in dazzling white clothing appeared. They just appeared. Didn't walk up the hill... didn't walk down the hill. They were just there. I recognized them, though! I had seen beings like them before... over 30 years earlier! I crouched behind a boulder, not wanting to interrupt the scene playing out before me. But I leaned forward and strained to hear what was being said.

"'Men of Galilee,' the new arrivals said, 'why do you stand here looking into the sky? This same Jesus, who has been taken from you into heaven, will come back in the same way you have seen Him go into heaven.' Then, as quickly as they had appeared, they vanished from sight.

"'Just wait. He will come!' My father's words echoed in my brain. The angels' voices rang out again... 'This Jesus *will* come back!'

"Well, I can tell you I didn't hesitate one more minute before joining that group of people. They invited me to come with them to discuss Jesus' life and teaching and to pray for Him to return. I learned from them that the baby I knew was indeed the same person I had just seen in the cloud. They explained that He had grown to become the kindest, wisest, most wonderful man... but that He was more than just a man. He was God's Son who had chosen to live life here on earth, so that He could fully identify with us human beings... feel what we feel, face what we face. And, though He was innocent of any wrong-doing, He was condemned like a criminal. He could have saved Himself from a horrific death but instead He chose to die, voluntarily accepting the punishment we humans deserve for our sins. Finally, I had caught up with Jesus. *Finally*, it all began to make sense!

"A short time later, I was with His followers when just as Jesus promised, the Holy Spirit came dramatically into our midst. That's another amazing story. I can assure you we were never the same again.

"So, over 30 years after that miraculous night on the hillside outside Bethlehem, I discovered that Jesus, the Messiah, had not come to deliver the Jews from Roman tyranny, but to deliver mankind, me included, from sin's tyranny. That is the greatest rescue in all of history! Better late than never, Jesus became my Friend."

General Nathaniel-Sir reached up, removed his shepherd's head-gear and laid down his staff and sling-shot. He paused and looked across the group of families gathered in the nursing home. It seemed he peered right at me and then, turned and fixed his gaze on Jeffrey.

"That is the end of my story," he said. "Of course we don't really know whether one of the shepherds ever played with Jesus when He was a baby, or if he met up with Him years later or was present at His ascension or Pentecost. But you can be sure those shepherds wondered whatever happened to that little baby they had found in a manger. Well, we know, don't we? Let me tell you, folks, that if you need a friend, ask Jesus and I guarantee He will come and be your best Friend. And one more thing... just as surely as He came in a wooden box over two thousand years ago, and as surely as He comes to live in us when we ask Him... He will come back again. Then we'll see Him in Person. And that is worth remembering and celebrating, not just at Christmas time, but all year long!"

Nate sighed. This had definitely been a different Christmas program, but he realized it was without doubt the best he had ever attended. He smiled as he surveyed the elderly residents in their makeshift, comical costumes, with walkers and wheelchairs, canes and crutches. He looked over at Jeffrey and his mother and realized that his hard heart towards his classmate had surprisingly been replaced with a tender heart of compassion. That, in itself, was like a little Christmas miracle. He caught General Nathaniel-Sir's eye as he walked to his seat, and gave the old gentleman a big grin. Nate just wished his father could have been there too.

Nate and his mom and little sister returned home and he could tell his mother's mood was brighter, just as his was. The program had reminded him that Christmas was about real people who dealt with tough, uncertain circumstances, just like he and his family were facing. He remembered the many times his father had assured him that Jesus was as close as a thought or a word. As Nate pulled on his pajamas and settled under his covers, he whispered,

"Jesus, I know You're really alive, even though I can't see You." He remembered Jeffrey's parting words on the bus and continued, "and I know my father is alive too, even though I can't see him. But You see him. Please watch over him this Christmas Eve, Jesus. And please help him to come back."

It was just a faraway voice in his dream at first. Nate rolled over in his bed and pulled his blanket tighter. The sound got louder. It was a voice... kind of scratchy, still far away, but definitely familiar. This wasn't a dream. This was real. Suddenly the scratchy voice came through loud and clear to Nate's awakening brain.

"Glory, Glory, Glory.... It's Christmas... Jesus is born! Wake up everybody. Let's celebrate!"

"Of course. Trust Mom to have made a recording of Dad's voice to play Christmas morning. Well, it's not the same as seeing him, but it surely is nice to hear the sound of his voice." Nate jumped out of bed and ran downstairs.

As he rushed into the living room, his mother was there waiting for his traditional hug, although it was one-armed since Amy Sue was clutched in her other arm.

"Merry Christmas, Nate," she smiled, then stepped aside. There, in front of the twinkling Christmas tree

where he always looked for his special gift, was a table with a brand new computer. And smiling from the wide flat screen... was his father!

"Dad!" he yelled.

"Good morning, sleepyhead. It's about time you got up. It sure is good to see you, even if it is via the wonder of technology."

"Wow, is it ever good to see you, Dad, and hear you too! Wow... Merry Christmas... Wow! I can't believe this!" His words tumbled out in excitement. He turned to his mom.

"Where did this set-up come from?" he asked. Their family had talked about getting a computer for some time but never felt they could afford one. "I mean, this is really expensive equipment." His mother pointed to the dining room.

"A rather special shepherd is responsible," she announced, and General Nathaniel-Sir, looking taller and more dignified than ever, stepped into the living room.

"Wow!" Nate exclaimed again. "Thank you so much. This is great!"

"Ummm, attention please, Nate...." It was his father's voice from the screen again. "Look under the table, Son." He was pointing downward. "I'd like to see you open the gift from your mother and me."

Nate hadn't even noticed the large package beneath the computer. He grabbed it and tore off the paper. It was a kit for the most amazing remote-control airplane he had ever seen. His face lit up, but then just as quickly clouded over.

"What's wrong, Nate?" his dad asked. "Don't you like it?"

"Sure, I love it Dad. I really do! It will be a fantastic plane, but I can't build something like that by myself. I'll have to wait until you come home."

"Oh no you don't. I want you to keep busy until I come. I think there's a certain General who would be more than happy to give you a hand."

"Would you, General Nathaniel-Sir?" Nathan turned to the white-haired commander.

"Certainly. I'd consider it an honor to work with such a fine young friend."

Nate picked up the large box. The pieces rattled inside. "Fine young friend." Nate liked the sound of that phrase. Suddenly he had an idea that even surprised himself.

"Could we start today?" he asked, but before the old gentleman could reply, Nate turned to his mother. "And Mom, could we invite Jeffrey and his mother over this afternoon? Maybe he would like to help us work on the plane too."

"Well, sure," his mother replied, "but do you think he'll come?"

Nate didn't know how he knew, but he just knew. Maybe it was what his father would call faith.

"Oh yes. Just wait. He *will* come."

Nate, Mom, Amy Sue and General Nathaniel-Sir chatted merrily with their beloved chaplain, until he told them he must sign off. He assured them he would make every effort to visit with them frequently via the computer.

"Nate," his father said, "you know I don't make promises I might not be able to keep. Each new day here holds dangers and uncertainties. I've told you that before. But I can promise you that Jesus is real. He came as a baby, He lived and died. And He's as alive this morning as you and I are. And one day He will come back for those of us who are His children. Just wait. He'll come... and then no matter what may have happened to us in this life, we will all be together for Christmas forever!"

"I know, Dad," Nate whispered. "Merry Christmas!" And with a tear-wet hand, he high-fived his dad through the screen.

Nate turned from the computer. This hadn't been such a bad Christmas after all. Jeffrey's words came back to his mind. Yes, there were risks, but Nate knew that he would trust Jesus no matter what happened to his father. And he couldn't help but feel excitement at the thought of becoming a friend to Jeffrey... perhaps even helping him come to know Jesus. After all, if Jesus made such a difference in the lives of all those people back in Bible times, surely He could change one bully on the school bus.

He turned to General Nathaniel-Sir who Nate would, forevermore, think of as a shepherd, and gave him a huge hug.

"Thank you so much for giving me my Dad for Christmas... even if he was in a box!" Nate laughed the merriest of Christmas laughs.

The shepherd-general rested his worn hand on Nate's shoulder.

"It was my pleasure, Nate. Merry Christmas! And don't you worry, son. Jesus is watching over your father. I believe he'll come back to you safe and sound. Just wait. Like Jesus... He will come!"

Nate grinned broadly... because somehow... he knew that too!

*...even though you do not
see Him now, you believe in Him
and are filled with an
inexpressible and glorious joy.*

1 Peter 1:8

Grandma's Whiskers

Tweezers! Oh horrors!

When Grandma approached me with tweezers in hand, I wanted to run and hide.

Ever since she and Grandpa came to live with us, she had chosen me as her personal whisker-plucker.

"Why me? After all, I'm just a kid," I reasoned.

But Grandma explained that I could see clearly and she couldn't. As far as she was concerned, that settled the question. I seriously considered faking vision loss. Why couldn't my mother do it? She was the woman's daughter. Or why not Grandpa? Surely a loving husband should help with such tasks. It seemed to me that yanking ugly hairs from an old lady's face was a sort of personal thing... the kind of job a grown-up should do. But Grandma wanted *me* and she had a way of always tracking me down, forcing those hated tweezers into my hands.

As a newly-turned adolescent, I had zero hair on my face and wondered why on earth my grandmother had such long strands protruding where a man's beard would grow. Was there something wrong with her? Obviously, I had never received an education about the aging process of male and female faces. Only years later did I discover that old people never really lose their hair. It just gets redistributed in odd places... earlobes, nostrils, eyebrows, and of course, chins!

Grandma had black strands popping out in numerous places on the bottom half of her face. They reminded me of a picture I'd seen once of a 13th century Mongolian warlord. Although, instead of sporting a long black pigtail, Grandma had a white one which was coiled and pinned neatly on the back of her head. The hair on her scalp was fine and wispy and gave a softness to her face. Only the chin hairs were black and coarse and vicious-looking... like the warlord's. Yes, I could see those hairs all too clearly.

If Grandma had lived today, I'm sure she would have heard about places where she could pay to have unwanted facial hair removed painlessly. But Grandma had never visited a beauty salon in her life. In fact, except for an occasional Sunday afternoon drive with my parents, she rarely left our house. So, a personal job like beard removal fell to me.

Perhaps if I had possessed more of a ruthless nature, the job wouldn't have been so bad. However, I was always afraid of hurting Grandma. She urged me to just go ahead and yank those hairs hard and fast. I know now that a quick jerk probably would have been the most painless way to remove them. But I worried about causing discomfort so, when I finally got a hair pinched between the prongs of the tweezers, I just pulled l-o-n-g and s-l-o-w. The result was that the flabby skin of her cheek would stretch out at least two or three inches from her face. I was terrified it would rip off along with the whisker. Creepy! It made me shiver.

When I pulled the hairs below her chin... ugh! That was even worse. Her neck was just like a turkey's. I felt like I was a poultry executioner! Grandma would kind of grimace while I was doing the long pull (thank goodness she never *gobbled).* Finally the hair would release. Then she would sigh and point to the next hair she wanted me to attack. I'd go through the whole ordeal again, until Grandma was sufficiently satisfied. I would hear her murmur, "Thank you Jesus!" as she hobbled away.

"Whoa, why are you thanking *Him?"* I'd wonder. *"I'm* the one doing the nasty job."

But Grandma thanked Jesus for lots of things. I would shrug and try to disappear before she discovered more hairs and returned for more tweezing. There were always plenty of strands still remaining on her face but she seemed content as long as I removed the peskiest ones. Within a few days, I knew she'd be back.

As Grandma sat in her big stuffed rocker for hours every day, she would rest her chin on her hand and stroke her cheek. That's when she would discover more bothersome hairs. Then she wouldn't rest until they were eliminated... by me.

I inwardly griped about this assignment, which continued throughout my early teen years. I complained regularly about it to my mother. She explained, over and over, that Grandma truly didn't see clearly enough to locate the unwanted strands, plus her hand wasn't steady or strong enough to manage the tweezers. It made me think of my grandmother as deficient and weak. I promised myself that, when I grew up, I would never get that way. I would always be strong and sharp enough to take care of myself. I would certainly *never* make any grandchild of mine pluck whiskers.

However, that attitude changed rather abruptly when I was 16... and it happened on Christmas night.

The whole year leading up to that Christmas had been tough. Grandma turned 85 and it seemed from that day on, her health began to decline. She became weaker and more frail with each passing month.

Grandma's Whiskers

Grandpa, on the other hand, was in excellent health. At 90, he was spry and strong. He bowled with other seniors and almost always won. Our house was full of his trophies. He did amazing woodworking projects in our basement. They were truly beautiful. The only problem was that, when they were finished, we had to find room for them in our house. You can only have so many lamps and end tables, wooden bowls, and candleholders until your home looks like a craft store. Grandpa rode the city bus downtown every week and, without fail, returned carrying a bouquet of gladiolas for Grandma. "Glads," as she called them, had always been her favorite flower. I thought it was sweet that after 60+ years of marriage, her husband would still do something so romantic.

This particular year though, Grandma didn't notice the flowers as much. Mom said she had "hardening of the arteries" and was becoming confused. She was tired and spent much of her time in bed. Her eyesight was worse, which meant even more plucking for me. All the adults in our extended family would talk quietly about her condition and I overheard my aunt say that she didn't think we'd have Grandma with us much longer. I wasn't sure whether that meant they were planning to move her out, or whether she was going to die, and I didn't want to ask.

Grandpa was as patient and loving towards her as always. I guess two people don't live together for so many years without feeling really connected. One day they were sitting in the living room. I overheard Grandma say,

"Ern, is it supposed to rain today?"

He answered, "No, I think it's supposed to be sunny."

"Oh, that's nice," Grandma replied.

They sat silent for a few minutes and then Grandpa said,

"Ida, I wonder if it's going to rain today."

She answered, "No, I think it's supposed to be sunny."

"Oh, that's good," Grandpa replied.

I thought I was losing my mind. Did they not just repeat the exact same conversation, only with their lines reversed? I concluded it wasn't just Grandma that was getting confused.

Summer arrived and Grandpa continued his many activities. Grandma mostly just sat or snoozed. Then one day Grandpa returned from an outing, coughing and wheezing. It seemed really hard for him to get his breath. After a few hours, the family decided to take him to the hospital. I never dreamed that 24 hours later my always-full-of-life Grandpa would be gone from us forever.

Grandma was too weak to attend the funeral. She cried a lot when my mom and my aunt told her that her beloved "Ern" had passed away and was now with the Lord. I avoided going anywhere near her room. It was really hard to see an old person crying like that. But then, after a weepy session, she would suddenly snap out of it. It was remarkable, really. She'd be cheerful and calm once again. I concluded maybe there was a good side to growing old and forgetful.

Fall came and went and before long Christmas was approaching. It was going to be different without Grandpa. He loved to buy presents and sign the tags, "From Santa." Of course we all knew that he had bought the gifts himself, but he got a kick out of pretending. It wouldn't be the same, without him putting his strands of bubbling-water lights and bunches of silver icicles on the tree. The whole family was missing him terribly and we all wondered how Grandma would handle this first Christmas without her sweetheart.

December 25 finally arrived. The air outside was cold and snow was forecast for later in the day. That would be nice. Since I had become a teenager, I didn't experience the hyper-excitement over Christmas that I had as a child, but still it was a special day. I liked celebrating the arrival of baby Jesus. I especially enjoyed the festivities and the food.

After breakfast Christmas morning, our whole family went into the living room to read the Christmas story from Luke 2 and Matthew 2. This had been our tradition for as long as I could remember. My father prayed, thanking God for the gift of Jesus. Then we were ready to begin opening gifts.

Suddenly, my grandmother who was sitting quietly in her overstuffed rocker, piped up.

"Where's Ern? We can't open gifts without Ern! Somebody needs to go call him."

We all sat silent. How should we respond? Grandpa had been dead for months. Grandma knew that but, obviously, she had forgotten. If we told her the truth, it would be like reliving his death all over again. She'd probably cry and cry. What a downer for Christmas day that would be.

My parents must have assumed Grandma would forget her question within a few minutes, so they said nothing and instead commenced the gift-opening. We got most of the presents unwrapped when Grandma piped up again, "Where's Ern? He shouldn't be missing this... go call him!" Again no one in the room responded.

The day wore on... turkey dinner, playing with

new games, trying on new clothes. Every hour or so Grandma would ask her question. She apparently was not going to let this subject drop. And she was becoming more and more agitated. For once, I was actually glad I was still considered a kid. I didn't have to handle this problem. But I was getting frustrated that the adults were just side-stepping the issue. I guess they just didn't know what to do.

By evening Grandma was provoked at Grandpa.

"Where is Ern? He's missed out on everything. He really needs to come here!"

The other adults gathered in the kitchen to discuss the situation.

"Finally," I thought. "Finally they're going to do something."

After several minutes of somber discussion, my mom and my aunt approached Grandma in her rocker and pulled chairs up on either side of her. They each took one of her hands in theirs and my aunt said gently,

"Mother, don't you remember that Dad died earlier this year? He's gone."

Grandma stared at her daughters for a long moment through those cloudy eyes of hers.

"Ern... he's gone? He died?"

"Yes."

She closed her eyes. She was quiet. Then two big tears rolled down her cheeks. They hung for a moment on a couple of her long chin hairs. But at that moment those hairs didn't seem so repulsive. I ached for Grandma.

We all sat silent, wondering what to do or say. All of a sudden, Grandma opened her eyes. They looked unusually clear and sparkling. Her wrinkly face, sprinkled with protruding whiskers, broke into a big smile.

"That means he's with the Lord!" she announced joyfully. "He's met our Savior. Ern's in heaven." She paused and her smile grew bigger. "I'll get to see him again! Someday soon I'll see him again. Oh, thank you Jesus!"

In that moment, Grandma ceased to be weak to me. She had an inner strength and simple faith that amazed me. Maybe it was Grandma who could see most clearly after all. I knew I was going to cry.

I went to the window and looked out. I was really just trying to get away where no one else would see the tears streaming down my face. Grandma was right... Christmas wasn't just about a baby... Christmas was about *heaven*. Christmas wasn't about the here and now. It was about *eternity*.

The snowflakes were falling and covering the bare ground with a glittering white. I thought about heaven and how Grandma would go there soon. She would see Grandpa. She would see her sweetheart once again. Better yet, she would be with the Lord. She'd be young and strong, clear-minded and clear-sighted. And never again would she need a single hair plucked!

"Thank You Jesus," I whispered. "Thank You for coming to earth to make a way to heaven."

I wiped the tears from my cheek and felt... what was that? My hand brushed across something rough on my face. It felt like... I rubbed it again. It was! A tiny stiff hair was poking out on my chin. I smiled and turned to go hunt Grandma's tweezers... this time, for *me*.

"Happy Birthday, Jesus." I said softly. "And..." I chuckled to myself, "I promise to never complain ever, ever again about my Grandma's whiskers!"

A Merry Christmas Postscript

Now that I'm a grandma myself, I have a greater appreciation for my grandmother's whisker dilemma. And though I could pay to have unwanted facial hair professionally removed, it does me good to stand in front of the mirror (a magnifying one, since my eyesight's not what it used to be!) and pluck away. It makes me remember those adolescent days when Grandma would seek me out with her tweezers in hand. What I'd give to be able to do that for her once again! Then I remember, with joy and thanksgiving, that she is in a much better place... with Jesus and Grandpa... and now my mom and dad and aunt and uncle as well. What a great time they must all be having together. And, just imagine... her cheeks and chin are hairless!

So, when Christmas rolls around, though I miss all those loved ones so much, I never wish them back. Instead, as I sing the carols, watch the special programs, and look at the nativity displays, I whisper, "Thank You Jesus. They're all with You, in heaven. Thank You for Your birth and death and resurrection which made that possible. And thank You that, someday, I too will join You and them forever."

The way I see it... *clearly* that's what makes Christmas very, very merry!

Christmas
Shoes

"**Y**ou stupid, stupid clumsy boy! Look what you've done!" Isabella jumped to her feet, as bright red punch soaked her sequined gown. "You've ruined my dress. Get out of here! Now!"

For 14 years old, Isabella could be a very demanding and intimidating child. But the object of her wrath, a lowly cook's helper, seemed unruffled.

"Very sorry, My Lady." The young man bowed politely. He set down the pitcher, now almost completely emptied of its contents, and tried to blot up the spilled liquid with the cloth he carried over his arm.

"Don't touch me, you fool! You shouldn't even be up here in the Nobleman's Hall. Get back to the castle scullery where you belong!"

Isabella's fury had attracted the attention of all the guests at the ball. The whole room was focused on the angry girl and the culprit, standing head down beside her.

A black-bearded man rose quickly from his table and strode across the room. He was dressed in a bold-colored tunic, decorated with a fine-woven dragon emblem on his chest. A gleaming sword hung by his side. The knight reached Isabella's table and took her firmly by the elbow.

"There, there, Isabella, you have many other gowns. You mustn't get so worked up. I have a great surprise for you tomorrow. It is Advent... only two days until Christmas... this is time for feasting and merry-making. You *must* calm yourself."

Then he whirled and glared at the guilty boy who had caused such a ruckus.

"You heard the maiden. You are a lowly, bumbling oaf! Get back to the kitchen immediately. I'll deal with you later."

Without a word, the servant bowed low again, turned and walked from the room. Then, squeezing Isabella's elbow even tighter, the knight escorted her to the door.

"Sir Drake, you're hurting my arm," Isabella winced.

"Stop making a scene, child," he hissed in her ear. "You will spoil tomorrow's surprise. Go to your room and change. Your attendant will find you another gown. I want you to look your best tonight. You certainly want to dance some more. I know you love dancing!"

Reluctantly, Isabella headed to her chamber at the other side of the great fortress. She was still finding her way around the enormous structure, having only recently arrived at Chillingham.

She was grateful for the man who had rescued her that dreadful night only a few weeks ago. He was stern, but he had showered her with all kinds of expensive clothing and trinkets. Still, she missed her parents terribly.

As Isabella walked the long stone passageways, she reviewed the events of that horrendous evening. Asleep in her bed, she had been suddenly awakened by a gloved hand clapped over her mouth. A dark figure loomed over her.

"Isabella... the castle is under siege! Your parents... your precious parents have been killed. Now you are in great danger. I promised your father I would get you to safety. Trust me, child!"

Wrapping a blanket around her and picking her up like a peasant's bundle, he carried her through the cavernous halls that had always been her playground. In an instant they had become black and foreboding. Terrified and confused, she closed her eyes and kept quiet.

All night and all the next day, she had ridden with Sir Drake, until finally they arrived at Chillingham. The castle was enormous, not as beautiful as her own dear Skipton Castle, but when Isabella saw the imposing tower and fortified walls, she knew she would be safe.

"You will be my daughter now," Drake had crooned as the girl sobbed. "I can never replace your own dear parents, but I will be a good father to you. You will see."

So far, he had kept his word. Anything Isabella wanted she got. Already a strong-willed, rather self-absorbed young lady, she didn't hesitate to make her wishes known. If Drake was willing to spoil her, so be it.

He had mentioned a surprise on the morrow. The girl began dreaming what delights might be awaiting her.

Isabella arrived at her quarters and, with the help of an elderly attendant, changed into a gorgeous holly-green silk gown, trimmed with lace and intricate beadwork. She selected an ornate, cone-shaped head-piece which looked stunning on her neatly-braided and beautifully-coiffed chestnut hair. Then, feeling suddenly rather chilled, she added a fur-trimmed satin cloak over her shoulders. Isabella looked down at her fancy embroidered leather shoes.

"Thank goodness he didn't get any punch on them," Isabella loved showing off fancy shoes and these were the showiest she had ever owned.

"Not the best for walking," she had to admit to herself, because their ridiculously-long pointed toes had to be stuffed with cloth to keep them straight and pre-vent the toes from folding under and sending the wearer sprawling.

Dismissing the servant, Isabella stepped over to her dressing table. She picked up a rectangular piece of polished brass, framed with gold filigree. Holding it in front of her, she surveyed her reflection and smiled with satisfaction.

"Maybe that stupid boy did me a favor," she thought. "I look even more beautiful now than I did before."

Laying the mirror back on the table, she turned to head back to the party. But, pausing at the door, she returned to the table, picked up the mirror and slid it into the pocket of her cape.

"Never know when this might come in handy to keep me looking my best," she said to herself and closed the heavy wooden door of her room behind her.

The young woman began to retrace her steps to the Great Hall but, as she turned the corner of the dimly-lit corridor, she was suddenly grabbed from behind. A muscular arm wrapped itself around her waist and a gloved hand clamped over her mouth. A male voice whispered in her ear,

"Don't say a word!"

Isabella opened her mouth and lunged forward, managing to bite the finger of her assailant.

"Ouch! You little tiger!" the voice muttered, but his hand tightened over her lips. He threw a hood over her head, then pushed her against the wall, whipped a cloth from his pocket and stuffed it into her mouth.

"Sorry, Isabella... but can't risk your shrieks bringing the whole castle after us."

Trying to dodge the pointed toes that were jabbing him in his shins, her assailant bound her wrists with a leather cord and hoisted her over his shoulder like a sack of potatoes. Another sack hung on his other shoulder, but neither load seemed to slow him down. He hurried in the opposite direction from the Great Hall, through a maze of passageways and finally out into the freezing cold December night.

Kicking and struggling, Isabella determined to not lose her new life and Sir Drake's generosity without a fight. She beat her captor's back with her fists, but the arms that held her just wouldn't let go. For the second time in just a few short weeks, she found herself being carried away!

Isabella's attacker plodded through the snow with his wriggling load for more than an hour. When he finally set his cargo down, he was breathing heavily.

They were now well into the forest, and only a thin shaft of moonlight illuminated the blackness. The villain lifted Isabella's hood. She blinked, trying to focus on her surroundings. Her gaze came to rest on the face in front of her. Her eyes widened in surprise and then flashed like daggers at her kidnapper.

"Isabella, I would be happy to take the gag from your mouth, but you have to promise that you won't start screaming. I really don't like screaming. Besides, there's no one around to hear you anyway... just me and the forest critters."

Isabella, eyes still glaring, nodded reluctantly and her captor gently removed the wadded-up piece of muslin.

"*You...* you stupid, stupid boy! How dare you think that you can get away with this. You fool... you belong in a dungeon!"

"Well, well, I do believe I heard similar words only a few hours ago. You really should develop a larger vocabulary."

There sitting cross-legged in front of Isabella, grinning mischievously, was the cook's helper who had doused her with punch at the ball.

"By the way, my name's Benny. Glad to finally meet you properly, Lady Isabella. Nice party hat!"

"You... you *kidnapper!*" Isabella hissed. "You can't keep me here. I order you to take me back to Chillingham!"

"Don't want to take you back." the servant replied.

"Sir Drake will come after me. He will rescue me. You're just a boy. You're no match for a strong knight like him!"

"True, I'm only 17 years old and your dear Sir Drake is a cunning warrior. But most assuredly, you don't want to go back to *him.*"

"Yes I do, and I am going to leave right now!" The feisty girl stood to her feet and looked around her.

"So, which path are you going to take?"

The girl took a step to her right, then stopped and looked to her left.

"Pretty dangerous for a pretty little thing like your-self to be wandering around in the middle of the woods on a frigid night."

Isabella realized how very cold she was and that she was in a helpless predicament. She really had no choice but to go along with this insane fellow... at least until daybreak, or until she had a reasonable chance of escape.

"All right. I guess I'm stuck with you for now. But it won't be long until Sir Drake sends his hounds after you and then you'll be dead as a fox!"

"Well actually, as far as the hounds... they're all enjoying the roasts I borrowed from the butler's pantry and doused with Sir Drake's own sleeping powder. I don't think they'll be chasing any foxes for awhile."

"Who in the world is this crazy young man?" Isabella wondered. "And what does he want with me?"

A kidnapping seemed like rather steep revenge for the tongue-lashing she had given him earlier. She surveyed his ragged clothes, worn boots and uncombed hair. She had never associated with servants before. They were far beneath her in importance.

"Come on Isabella. I want to put some more distance between us and Chillingham by daybreak. You can stay here and take your chances with a bear but, if you ask me, the safest place in these woods is right beside me."

Benny reached out and untied her leather cuffs. Taking her by the hand, he helped her to her feet.

"Follow me!"

The pair hiked snow-covered trails for several more hours. Isabella's mind raced the whole time.

"Where was this Benny taking her? Was he part of a band of thieves? Was he planning to use her as bait for a hefty ransom?"

She knew Sir Drake would pay any price to get her back. Shivering, she was glad she had grabbed her cape, as an after-thought. She would have been frozen solid without it and the sharp-edged mirror, still hidden in her pocket, might very well serve as a handy weapon at some point.

The fashionable shoes she had greatly admired a short time before, made walking painfully difficult. Isabella felt blisters developing. She had planned to dance the night away at the Advent Ball. Now she was trudging through the forest with this demented youth.

Finally Benny stopped and pointed ahead. Isabella strained to see what he was pointing at.

"We can rest in that cave for a few hours. I know you're growing weary."

Isabella didn't relish spending any time alone in a cave with this stranger, but she was exhausted and couldn't wait to get off her sore feet. As she entered the dark cavern, Benny set down the pack he had carried all night and removed from it a small bundle of kindling. He began rubbing two twigs together. In a few minutes he had started a fire... definitely not a roaring blaze,

but enough of a flame to warm their hands. Isabella kicked off her shoes and massaged her aching feet. Then removing her ornate "party hat," as Benny had called it, she rolled it into a ball for a makeshift pillow. Though she was determined not to fall asleep with this good-for-nothing criminal beside her, she soon drifted off.

Benny leaned his head against the rocky wall of the cave, but kept watch all night.

When rays of sunlight finally brightened the entrance of their shelter, the captor shook the sleeping girl.

"Wake up Isabella. We need to get going."

"Where am ...?" Then she remembered with a shudder the events of the previous evening.

"You're not going to get away with this, you idiot!"

Benny just smiled. Once again he reached into his pack and pulled out another bundle, not wood this time, but cloth. He tossed it to Isabella.

"Your clothes aren't much good for hiking," he said. "Change into these. I'll step outside."

"And what if I refuse?" Isabella retorted.

"Then you can keep catching that satiny gown on briars and nettles and tripping over it every few steps. This stuff will make a march through the glade a lot easier. But do what you want."

He walked to the mouth of the cave and turned his back.

Isabella took stock of the rough woolen skirt and heavy tunic. She knew they made a lot more sense than her lavish gown and cape. Not used to dressing or un-dressing unassisted, she struggled to unhook the many buttons and clasps of her outfit, but finally managed to get into the new attire. Checking to make sure Benny was still looking away, she pulled the mirror from her cape and scrutinized her image. Her hair was in tousled disarray from hours on the cavern floor. She unfastened her jeweled hair pins and let her hair fall disheveled to her shoulders. A smudge of soot streaked her cheek. She tried to wipe it away, but only added more dirt to her face. She frowned disgustedly as she took stock of her raiment... clothes of a pauper... dull, plain and stained. She had never worn such rags in her life. But she had to admit they were definitely warmer than her silks. Her pointed-toe shoes looked ridiculous with such an outfit. Benny's fashion taste evidently hadn't included footwear. Isabella sighed, folded her expensive garments into a bundle and brought them to Benny.

"Put these in your pack," Isabella ordered. "I'm not getting rid of them!"

"Then I guess you will have to carry them," Benny replied matter-of-factly, "because I don't intend to carry around your old clothes." He slung his pack over his shoulder, took her hand and half led, half dragged her from the cave.

All morning, Isabella whined and complained about her clothes, her shoes, the snow, Benny's singing… that really irritated her! He sang or hummed incessantly! She told him he sang like a crow.

"You whine too much, Isabella." Benny grinned. "Personally I like to think I have the voice of a *dove.*" Isabella laughed disdainfully at that as the two kept walking.

By the time the sun had long passed overhead, Isabella was tired, cranky and extremely hungry. She hadn't eaten anything since the banquet the night before and that had been rudely interrupted by Benny's clumsiness. She complained to him that he was starving her to death. The pair had just come to a clearing at the crest of a hill and, looking into the valley, they could see a small village a short distance ahead.

"I'm sure we can find some food there," Benny stated.

"How do you expect to get food?" Isabella asked. "I'm sure you have no money."

"I'll figure something out," Benny promised.

As they neared the outskirts of the town, a farmer approached them with a cart laden with turnips and potatoes.

"How much for four potatoes?" Benny asked.

"Two half-pennies," the farmer replied.

"Would you take this instead?" Before Isabella knew what was happening, Benny had snatched her bundle of fancy clothes and held it out to the farmer.

The peasant gave a whistle.

"Well, now, I'll even throw in a couple of turnips for that. Won't my missus think she's died and gone to the gates of Paradise, when she sees finery like this!"

"Wait!" Isabella protested, but Benny had already popped four potatoes and two turnips into his bag and was pulling her toward the town.

Benny led his unwilling companion to the village church, an imposing stone structure easily spotted at the end of a dirt street.

Entering through the carved archway, Isabella surveyed the lovely sanctuary. An amazing stained-glass Jesus looked down from the front of the nave. An abundance of pine boughs and holly graced the altar table. Benny led her to a wooden pew.

"We can rest here a bit," he announced, "and eat our potatoes too."

"*Raw* potatoes?" Isabella fumed.

"What's wrong with that?" Benny asked. "Just be thankful you have something to eat."

"I'm not thankful for anything right now," Isabella complained. "I'll only be thankful when Sir Drake comes to free me from you!"

"Why do you keep believing that he will come for you?" Benny asked.

"Because he cares for me. He rescued me from being slaughtered like my parents, when our castle was attacked. Sir Drake took me to Chillingham and gave me wonderful gifts. In fact, he vowed to give me a great surprise today! Of course you've ruined that," she grumbled.

"Yes, well, about that... it was going to be a surprise all right. But not the kind you were expecting. I over- heard Sir Drake bargaining with a despicable warrior from Scotland... a cruel and evil scoundrel of a man. Your great knight was planning to sell you for a bag of gold shillings! The deal was set to happen today."

"You're lying!" Isabella shouted.

"I don't lie," Benny responded. "And definitely not in church. You thought Sir Drake was your deliverer but he was really about to destroy your life forever."

"I don't believe you!" Isabella insisted.

"Fine," Benny replied. "But truth will surface like oil on water. You'll see."

"Time to move on," Benny announced to Isabella when she had finally managed to choke down a good portion of the potato he had peeled for her.

"I want to put more distance between us and that fiend of a knight."

"I can't walk another ten steps in these shoes," Isabella fussed. "They're killing me!"

"I always wondered why women and girls wear such foolish things on their feet," Benny commented. "You can barely walk in them. I can't imagine that you can dance in them."

"What would you know about dancing?" Isabella retorted. "You're just a slave. I bet you've never been to a proper dance in your life. And when Sir Drake finds us, your days will be over. No dancing *ever* for you. You'll be dead for sure!"

"Actually, I'm as good of a dancer as I am a singer."

He chuckled, leaped in the air, clicking his heels to-gether and began singing a rousing Yuletide carol.

"Oh, be quiet! We're in *church.*" Isabella scolded. But her voice wasn't so sharp and she had to look away from Benny to hide the upturned corners of her mouth.

The two took to the road once again. The forest now behind them, they had easier going on the rutted roads. But the afternoon sun was beginning to dip, the air was growing colder and snowflakes had begun to fall.

By dusk, they were approaching a tiny hamlet. As they grew closer, sounds of music and laughter greeted them.

"What's going on?" Isabella wondered aloud.

"Well, it is Christmas Eve," Benny reminded her. "Peace on earth. Good will toward men. All that nice stuff. You do know about that don't you?"

"Of course I do. I'm not a heathen."

"Could have fooled me," Benny quipped.

Entering the tiny community, the weary couple couldn't help but sense the air of celebration. In the courtyard right in the center of town, dozens of peas-ant folk danced and sang. Benny spied a girl about Isabella's age dancing a rollicking jig on the edge of the crowd. He made a beeline towards her, pulling Isabella with him.

"Excuse me miss, but would you be willing to trade your footgear for these fine specimens my dear sister is wearing?"

Startled, the young girl stared down at the long pointy toes of Isabella's shoes. In a flash, she removed her scuffed and dirty boots and held them out to Isabella.

Benny tipped his head in the direction of Isabella's feet as if to say, "Get a move on girl!"

Rolling her eyes at Benny, Isabella stooped over, pulled the tortuous shoes from her feet and exchanged them for the cowhide boots.

"How do they fit?" Benny asked. "How do they feel?"

"Well, they're ugly and stinky but, they fit perfectly and they feel even better than perfect, after those horribly uncomfortable toothpicks I've been wearing! I guess maybe I should thank you, Benny."

"You're very welcome, lovely Isabella. Would you care to dance? Remember, I dance just as well as I sing." Benny held out his hand towards her with a dramatic bow.

Isabella's feet had never felt so light. She looked at the simple folk, laughing, singing and twirling around her. She had never witnessed such joy at the most lavish balls she had attended. She was puzzled at the good time she was beginning to have with this Benny... but it was Christmas, so why not indulge in a bit of gaiety? She would be angry with him again later.

The music gradually softened and, at one point, a villager stepped from the doorway of a simple cottage. He walked confidently across the courtyard and climbed up on a wagon in the center of the festivities. Spying him, a bystander gave a loud whistle and silenced the crowd.

"We're listening to you, Parson!" he shouted. "Go ahead!"

The man on the wagon lifted a lantern high and began,

"And there were in the same country, shepherds abiding in the fields, keeping watch over their flocks by night..." In a voice more compelling than any castle cleric, he quoted the gripping narrative from Saint Luke.

Isabella and Benny stood hushed with the rest of the humble townspeople, all of them savoring the reverent moment. Isabella looked at Benny and smiled reluctantly. She felt herself almost wanting to trust this lowly cook's helper.

But the perfect moment was abruptly shattered by the sound of pounding horses' hooves. Benny grabbed Isabella and, in a flash, pulled her into the parson's "cottage."

"Benny, what's happ...?" Isabella blurted.

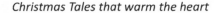

"Sshhh!" Benny commanded. The horses thundered into the courtyard. Isabella and her captor scrunched down by a window and peered cautiously over its sill. The riders were dressed in full armor, fearsome swords by their sides. The leader dismounted and approached the villager who had just recited the glorious Biblical account.

Benny and Isabella couldn't hear their conversation. But they saw the knight draw his sword and point the tip menacingly at the center of the poor man's chest. More words were spoken as the preacher waved his hands and shook his head from side to side. Finally, the dark knight slid his weapon back into its sheath and turned to remount his black stallion. In a thin slice of moonlight, Isabella caught a sudden glimpse of the golden dragon on his shield.

"Sir Drake!" she gasped. About to leap from their hiding place, she felt Benny's hand gently on her arm and hesitated. Their eyes locked.

"Isabella," Benny whispered. "Call out to him if you want. You may leave if you wish. But I am warning you. You will find nothing good with him."

Isabella's heart quarreled within her. She knew it came down to a matter of trust. Which man was telling the truth? Which one should she believe?

Benny held her gaze for what seemed like an eternity. Finally, the young woman's eyes filled with tears.

"All right. You win. I choose you, Benny!" she whispered. "What I'm getting myself into, I don't know... but I choose you!"

Benny grinned that impish grin of his.

"You won't be sorry. I promise."

Somehow Isabella sensed that this promise was different than Sir Drake's. The pair remained crouched by the window until the battalion of soldiers rode away.

"Come on, we need to find a place for the night!"

As they rose to leave, they realized for the first time that their place of refuge was not a dwelling at all, but rather a charming little chapel. No stained-glass or ornate furnishings like the towering church in the bigger town... just a few backless benches facing a simple wooden altar table. Displayed on it was a delicately-carved nativity scene. No garlands of pine or holly or festive ribbons. But the pair was drawn to it and couldn't help but run their fingers over the beautiful figures.

"Now this is my kind of church." Benny whispered.

Finally leaving the hallowed little place of worship, and keeping in the shadows, the two made their way down narrow alleys towards the edge of the village.

"We don't dare go any farther on the road tonight," Benny warned. "Sir Drake and his men are too close. And we don't want the townsfolk to spot us either, lest one of them get the idea of turning us in. We need to find a place to lay low."

At the end of the narrow side street, he spied a deserted shed. Entering cautiously, the two surveyed their one-room ramshackle hideout. It was filthy, cobwebs everywhere. A couple of rats scurried into the dark corners. Some old barrels smelled of stale whiskey and mold. Isabella shivered.

"Definitely not a castle," she thought to herself. Aloud, she said,

"This will do fine, Benny. Actually, it's probably better than baby Jesus had on Christmas Eve." She laughed and swept her arm dramatically around the room. Inwardly, she was amazed and puzzled at the change in her attitude. Less than 48 hours before, she would have recoiled from such a place. She would have demanded a perfect room and bed. Now, those things just didn't seem to matter much.

The two used a couple of old boards to sweep away little bits of straw and brush that were scattered here and there on the dirt floor. Then Benny pulled out another little bundle of twigs and worked his magic to produce a wee fire. Isabella stepped to the open window and gazed up at the stars.

She still wasn't totally sure she had made the right decision to stay with Benny. She fingered the mirror in her pocket. It could yet become a handy weapon, if needed. But when she looked towards Benny, he grinned at her in the firelight and her expression softened.

"Blessed Christmas Eve, Isabella! Now you better get some sleep."

Isabella lay down once again by the fire but, unlike last night, tonight she would sleep in peace.

Christmas Day dawned crisp and cold. Snowdrifts were piled up along the side of their shack.

"Come on Isabella. Today, we reach our destination."

"You haven't even told me where we're going."

"And I'm not going to… at least not yet. But I can promise you a nice Christmas present later today."

Isabella glanced around the run-down shed. She almost hated to leave it.

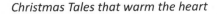

"Well, I'm sorry I don't have a Christmas present for you, Benny. After all, I wasn't exactly expecting this trip!" Her fingers touched the expensive mirror in her pocket. "No, that won't do. Boys don't care about mirrors," she reasoned. But it gave her an idea.

"Benny, could we make a short stop on our way out of town?"

"Sure, but where? What's your idea?"

"You'll see!" This time, Isabella led the way back to the center of town. She was thankful that, being Christmas Day, folks were not out on the streets. They were undoubtedly celebrating in their homes with their families. A wave of sadness swept over her, as she recalled the many lavish Christmases she had enjoyed with her parents at Skipton. Those days were gone forever. What lay ahead she didn't know, but she resolved that she would not get stuck mourning her lost past. Arriving at her destination, she motioned Benny to follow her into the tiny chapel that had been their hiding spot the night before.

Entering the hushed chamber, Isabella removed the valuable mirror from her pocket. It glistened in a ray of sunlight that penetrated the darkened room. She raised it and did a swift perusal of her appearance.

"Definitely shabby." she announced.

"No... not shabby... *beautiful.*" Benny murmured.

Isabella shot him a grateful smile. Then, approaching the altar, she placed the costly polished brass with its intricate gold filigree in front of the carved nativity scene.

"Jesus will know how to put this to good use," she stated confidently. "Now, Benny, what's my surprise?"

Benny grabbed her by the hand. Isabella felt like the shepherds must have felt on their way to Bethlehem... looking for something, someone, some place... not exactly sure what they would find. Her excitement was mounting.

They trudged through the snow for a couple of hours. The crisp winter air filled their lungs. Isabella joined Benny in singing every Christmas carol they knew. Halfway through a last chorus of "Glo...o...o... o...ria," they came over the knob of a hill and Benny pointed to a gray speck on the horizon.

"There's your Christmas surprise!" he announced.

Isabella shaded her eyes and squinted. She tilted her head and strained to see what Benny was pointing to. She gasped.

"Skipton. It's Skipton Castle... my home!" She shook her head vehemently. "No, Benny. I don't want to go there. It will be nothing but ruins! It was attacked and plundered that night weeks ago. Even if I could salvage a few belongings, my parents won't be there!" Her voice broke. Her excitement had crashed dismally, just as quickly as it had been aroused.

"Didn't I tell you Sir Drake is a liar?" Benny chided. "Come on. Your Skipton Castle is just fine!"

Running, slipping, sliding and laughing, the two covered the distance to the castle walls faster than jack rabbits. In no time at all, the gates lifted and two crying parents came running, arms open wide to welcome their daughter home!

Finally, Isabella heard the truth. There had been no attack on the castle. Her parents had not been murdered. It was Sir Drake's evil plot all along to kidnap the girl and sell her for a hefty sum. Her parents had been sick with fear for their daughter's fate. They thought they had lost her forever.

Now Isabella watched them bow before the peasant boy in gratitude. But he pulled them to their feet.

"Thank you is good enough." he said. "And maybe a bit of a party!"

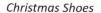

What a Christmas celebration that was. There was feasting and dancing and merrymaking the rest of the day. Isabella and Benny in their peasant garb and her parents and all the lords and ladies in their finery... but no one seemed to notice the difference.

When evening came, Isabella realized that she was completely exhausted and bid a fond goodnight to her parents. But before she headed for her room, she had to see Benny.

"How can I ever thank you?" she asked. "I didn't want to trust you. I fought you. But you saved my life. With all my heart, I thank you Benny!"

"Gratitude becomes you." Benny beamed. "I'm just glad I could help. Good night Isabella. And Merry Christmas!"

"Merry Christmas, Benny!"

Isabella slept soundly and long in her very own soft bed. Awakening only when the sun shone brightly into her room, she ran to her mother and father's room. She pounced on them and wrapped her arms around them.

"It is so good to be home!" she murmured. Then suddenly remembering her friend,

"I wonder what Benny and I can find to do today? Have you seen him yet this morning?"

Her mother put her arm on Isabella's shoulder.

"Actually, Benny left late last night, dear."

"What? Why? How could you let him leave? He just got here. He may be just a commoner, but that didn't mean you had to get rid of him. You didn't need to kick him out! You should have *knighted* him and given him the highest position in the castle! How could you send him away?"

"We didn't make him go." Her father spoke gently. "And we couldn't make him a knight, even if we wanted to."

"Why not? Just because he was a poor servant?" Isabella accused, a mixture of angry and broken-hearted tears now streaming down her face.

"We couldn't make him a knight, because Benny is already a Prince. Prince Benedictus, son of the King."

"What?" Isabella blinked tearfully. "Benny is royalty?"

"Yes. He most assuredly is. When we discovered you missing that terrible morning, your father sent a message to the King, pleading for help. His Highness devised the daring rescue plan and his son volunteered to carry it out. We will be forever thankful for the valiant courage of that young man! But my dear, before he left, Prince Benedictus left you a Christmas gift."

Her mother pointed to a burlap-wrapped box on a table across the room.

Isabella hurriedly untied the leather cords. Eagerly lifting the lid of the box, she peered inside. There lay a pair of shoes... simple, doeskin slippers, delicate, light as feathers, with the slightest bit of a point on the toes. Isabella couldn't help but grin as she picked them up tenderly and caressed the soft leather. As she did, she heard the rustle of paper. Reaching into one of the shoes, she withdrew an envelope addressed with her name. Trembling, she turned it over, and caught her breath as she saw the wax seal of the monarchy.

Gingerly breaking the seal, Isabella unfolded the note and read the brief but to-the-point message, written by her rescuer, her servant Prince...

Dear Isabella,

I am sorry I had to leave. I have some kingdom business to attend to. But don't worry! I'll be back. And when I come, we'll dance again. Yes. We will dance!

Love always,
Benny

P. S. Merry Christmas and welcome home!

His government and its peace
will never end.
He will rule with fairness and justice
from the throne of his
ancestor David for all eternity.
The passionate commitment
of the LORD of Heaven's Armies
will make this happen!

Isaiah 9:7 (NLT)

Twelve Days of Christmas

Isabella slipped quietly from the Great Hall, crowded with servants who were dancing, feasting and boisterously enjoying their Christmas merrymaking. Normally the lovely 19-year-old would have joined in the partying, especially the lively jigs and elegant waltzes. However, tonight her heart just wasn't into celebrating. Days ago, her parents were called to the aid of an ailing relative on the mainland, leaving Isabella in charge of the castle over the holidays. She was grateful for their trust and was doing her best to provide truly jolly events for the castle staff and their families. But she was weary of the noise and just couldn't muster up much Yuletide joy. She retreated to her chambers in the "keep" of the fortress, which was her home. Closing the door, she plopped wearily at her desk and picked up the most recent letter from Benny... the love of her heart.

Five years had passed since that Christmas when Benny had rescued her from Sir Drake, a villain of the worst sort. Isabella smiled at the memory. How fiercely she had fought Benny's efforts to save her. How patiently he had persevered to get her to safety. And how absolutely amazed she was to finally discover that

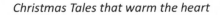

her deliverer was not an impudent peasant, but actually Prince Benedictus, son of their beloved King.

"Oh, m' Lady! I'm so sorry. I just noticed thee had left the ball. Art thou ill? Can I bring thee something? Friar Jon says that laughter is an excellent tonic. Maybe thee shouldst go back to the party..."

A rust-haired young woman, only a year Isabella's junior, had burst into the room and rushed to her mistress' side. Shorter and a little rounder than the beautiful Isabella, she was a perky and pretty lass. Her plump hand reached out to feel her employer's forehead.

"I'm fine, Marelee. Really I am." Isabella insisted.

This spirited girl had been her personal attendant for only a few months. When her mother announced she had hired a woman to attend to her daughter's daily needs, Isabella had expected a gray-haired matron. She was shocked to be presented instead, with this cheery and very chatty peer.

"But Marelee, I've had enough Christmas frivolity. I just want to be quiet."

Marelee glanced at the folded paper in Isabella's palm.

"Yes m'Lady. I understand completely. Thou art surely missin' thy prince tonight. Friar Jon says that absence makes a heart of true love, long powerf'ly."

"Ah yes, I believe Friar Jon is quite accurate about that."

Isabella had resigned herself weeks ago to the fact that her handmaid couldn't help quoting this saintly cleric in practically every verbal exchange. Soon after starting her service to Isabella, Marelee shared that Friar Jon had come to the rescue of the peasant girl and her siblings, when their parents died of a fever. If it hadn't been for his frequent visits, his gifts of food and clothing, and his wise counsel, the girl was certain every one of them would have died of starvation or sorrow.

"I don't know how he did it," Marelee had explained, "but Friar Jon seemed t'know just when we was needin' help and then... there he'd be! He still stops by our wee hamlet from time t' time and sits and talks like we was the only people needin' help in the whole of England."

A sudden sharp knock startled both girls. Isabella gave a nod to Marelee who cautiously cracked the chamber door and peered into the dark corridor. With a gasp of surprise, the servant turned back to her mistress.

"It's Sir Jephridous, m'Lady!"

"Well, invite him in, of course!" Isabella instructed. The tall, handsome knight was her Benny's trusted assistant. He rarely left the side of the Prince, except when asked to hand-deliver a letter to Isabella. Marilee ushered the young man into the sitting room.

"Sir Jephridous, please come in. A very merry Christmas to you. And..." Isabella couldn't hide her eagerness. "Would you happen to have any word from the Prince?"

"Thank you, Lady Isabella. A very merry Christmas to you as well. And please, you may call me Jeph. That's what the Prince calls me."

He gave barely a glance at Marelee who stood awestruck in the presence of such a man of distinction, in spite of the fact that he could barely be more than a couple of years her senior. He stepped towards Isabella and handed her an envelope, clearly sealed with the royal insignia.

"A sincere thanks to you, Jeph, for bringing this." Isabella had to admit to herself that, if her heart were not so totally smitten with Benny, this soldier could seem quite appealing. "Will you stay at the castle for a few days and join in our Christmas celebrations?"

"My deepest gratitude, m'Lady, for such a gracious invitation but I must leave tonight to return to the Prince. Drake and his armies have been wreaking havoc in many villages. We anticipate more attacks this week and Prince Ben is bound to stop him. We believe we are very close to capturing him and putting a stop to his shenanigans. So the Prince and I have a busy week ahead. But I know His Highness plans to be at his father's on the sixth of January to celebrate Epiphany."

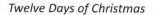

"In that case, Marelee, take Jeph to the cook and see that he gets a good hearty meal. Then, if you don't mind, Jeph, please come back to me before you leave. I will write a reply to Benny and you can deliver it to him, if you would be so kind."

With a nod, the two disappeared down the passageway and Isabella tore open the precious letter. As her eyes travelled down the page, she felt her heart beating faster and faster. The smile, absent from her face only a few minutes earlier, now returned in splendor as she read and re-read the question she had been hoping, for months, to be asked. Reaching for paper and quill, she began to write...

"My dearest Benny, my Prince... Yes! Yes! Yes!..."

Isabella and Marelee climbed into the little skiff and, grabbing the oars, the servant propelled the vessel out into the frigid waters of the D'Argent River. It was December 28. They were on their way to surprise Benny at Bailederi Hall, the residence of his monarch father.

Within hours after Benny's aide had left her on Christmas night, Isabella had hatched her plan. She and Marilee would head to the King's castle too, and arrive well before the festivities on January 6.

"Marelee, it will be a marvelous way to celebrate the coming of the wise men to the Christ Child," Isabella had coaxed. "You know Epiphany is the highlight of the Advent season and I so want to experience it with Benny! My parents are away anyway, and the castle steward can easily take care of things while we are gone. The Prince has asked me to *marry* him, Marelee. I *must* see him! I am only listening to the love in my heart and certainly that can't be wrong."

"Mmmph. Friar Jon would say, 'a heart of love still needs to listen to a head of sense.'"

"Marelee, watch your words. You are, after all, paid to do my bidding. This makes perfect sense to me."

"Yes, m'Lady. Please forgive me. It's just that…"

Isabella shot a warning glare and Marelee lowered her eyes in submission.

"We'll need a day to get affairs in order here and another day to prepare for the trip. We'll need some heavy woolen clothing… peasant garb, so as to not draw attention. And we should each take a small bag with a gown suitable for our destination. I calculate the journey itself will take about three days. We can be there by the New Year."

"Actually, m'Lady, if we was to go by river rather than road, t'would be a day shorter. The road east to Bailederi winds up and down and twists terrible. We'd be goin' a mighty long way 'round t'get there. My village is only an hour north from here, and I can get us a boat there. Then it's a straight float east to the King's house."

"That sounds like a wonderful plan. Let's do it!"

So here they were, gliding peacefully down the river, the water shimmering around them in the light of the late December sun. Marelee, obviously strong and experienced, managed the oars. Isabella patted the precious letter, tucked into a pocket of her cape. She opened the leather bag at her feet and ran her fingers over the doeskin shoes Benny had given her years ago. She had saved them for the day when she would dance with him, as his wife. Now, here she was, on the brink of marriage. Her heart was bursting over the prospect of being with Benny. She hummed contentedly and then, with a grin and a melodramatic sweep of her hand, began to sing,

"Row, Girl, row this boat... speedily down this stream... oh Marelee, oh Marelee, isn't life a glorious dream?"

The rower burst out laughing.

"M'Lady, I b'lieve thee could be England's new bard. Such a ditty could be catchin'. Although, Friar Jon says our best dreams t'aint nothin' t'all compared to what the Almighty likes t'do for His children."

"He's right Marelee. God certainly outdid Himself when He brought Benny into my life. What about you, Marelee? Do you have a dream?"

The russet curls bobbed up and down.

"Oh yes. Me had a best chum when we was just urchins. But he grew up and moved away t' better things. Friar Jon says if God takes somethin' away He brings it back again or somethin' even better. So that's what I'm awaitin' on." The servant giggled and began pulling even harder on the oars.

The hours passed and soon the fading light alerted the young women that they would need to find a place to spend the night. Scanning the shoreline, Isabella spotted a wood and straw structure at the top of a path that wound its way into the forest. Marelee guided the boat into the tall reeds and they climbed the bank to the abandoned shack backed up against the thicket. It wasn't much, but the hut was roomier than they expected and it would provide much-welcomed shelter from the cold.

Inside, Marelee produced some bread and cheese and a flask of water. The two adventurers admitted that this meal tasted better than many fancy banquets back at the castle.

"Friar Jon says luxury has more t'do with companions than possessions," the servant girl quipped.

"My gracious, you amaze me with your quotes, Marelee. You are quite an interesting person. And, I've been meaning to ask just how you got your name. I've never heard of anyone else named Marelee."

"Well, m'Lady, me mother said she wanted to call me 'Merrily' bein' as she wanted a happy child. But me folks never did learn their letters and when she told the magistrate m'name, he wrote it down as 'mare' and 'lee.' So, I'm part female horse and part shelter from the wind."

"Well, I think you should get your name changed to its intended spelling," Isabella declared.

"Oh, no need, m'Lady," Marelee replied. "Friar Jon says 'thy name is how thou lives it, not how thou writes it.' So, I try to live on the happy side... not the horsey side."

The two travelers giggled together like 12-year-olds and, using their bags for pillows, settled down to sleep in the now-almost-pitch-black room.

"Marelee," Isabella whispered after a few moments. "This journey makes me think of the Magi on their way to find the newborn King. I wonder if they also went to sleep on a night like this, dreaming of what the next few days would bring. Oh, Marelee, I'm so content. It may be dark in here, but truly all is calm and all is bright in my heart."

Her companion murmured sleepy agreement but, as she drifted to sleep, from far back in her memory came Friar Jon's words, "Beware... thine enemies do their worst work in the dark."

The nightmare erupted just before dawn. The sound of horses' hooves, like an approaching tempest, jolted the girls from their sleep.

"Quick," Marelee hissed. "We've got t'flee. Grab thy sack. We'll hide in the reeds by the river."

In a daze, Isabella staggered to her feet and slung her bag over her head. But as Marelee cracked the door, their eyes were blinded by what seemed like a wall of torches before them. Five churlish knights with blazing lights forced open the door and burst into the room. Though the young women struggled valiantly, they were no match against brute strength. Within seconds, both girls' arms were held fast by four foul-smelling, grizzly-looking soldiers. Isabella recognized the horrid dragon symbol on their armor and shuddered... Drake's men.

The apparent leader lifted his torch higher, illuminating his diabolic features. It was a face etched forever in Isabella's memory... Drake himself! Her terror mounted.

"My, oh my... quite the lovely lassies we have here... just the company we tired gentlemen need," the fiendish voice gloated. He stepped closer to Isabella and ran his rough hands over her cape. The crackle of her precious letter caught his attention. Reaching into her pocket, he withdrew the envelope and, spotting the royal seal, quickly scanned the letter. A sinister smile formed on his lips.

"Well, well, well... I do believe it is the lovely Lady Isabella who has fallen into my clutches. I didn't even recognize you in your pauper's garb. Quite a stunning woman you are now. Not that scrawny rat I knew years ago."

"Why you...!" Marelee struggled to free herself from her captors, but they held her fast.

"Oh, such a loyal slave you have here. How pitifully noble that she would try to protect you. Seems you have a way of attracting gallant rescuers, Isabella. Unfortunately for you though, I don't think this pudgy little worm can help you tonight. Here I thought my men and I had just found a convenient spot to rest our weary bones and enjoy a little Yuletide ale, but it looks like we've landed a much bigger prize."

"Change of schedule, men. I planned, at daybreak, to scout out another village to add to our conquests but it appears we have the Prince's bride-to-be right here before us... just the bait our army needs to ensnare

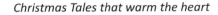

him. Once we have *him*, we'll have what we need to lure the King himself into our trap. I may be on the throne even sooner than anticipated. What a merry Christmas season this is turning out to be for *me!*" He chuckled sadistically. "Bring her along. We need to ride back to the main road and rejoin the rest of the troops. Then we can set our trap."

"What about this one?" one of the ruffians asked, shoving Marelee forward.

"Oh, no need for her."

Like a sudden streak of lightening, Drake whirled, swinging his iron-clad arm brutally into the side of the unsuspecting girl's head. The crack was sickening and the battered victim crumpled to the ground.

Marelee!" Isabella screamed. Already she saw the girl's blood spilling from beneath her red tresses. "Marelee! Marelee!" Isabella cried as she was dragged from the hut. "Oh, Marelee, what have I done?"

The savage men lifted their prisoner onto a horse and bound her hands tightly to the saddle pommel. Her tears ran hot and her heart broke in anguish as she watched the soldiers shut the door and then prop a torch against it. Within seconds the place that, only moments ago, had been their sweet haven, was now a raging fiery tomb. Isabella sobbed. Her friend, her precious friend, was dead and, along with her, had perished both girls' beautiful dreams!

As captors and captive rode swiftly down the trail, Isabella wept inconsolably. Drake and his cold-blooded henchmen savored devilish thoughts of their anticipated conquest. But as they thundered down the path, none of them spotted the hooded figure that stepped silently from the shadows.

A very eager prince, along with his right-hand man, rode up to Skipton Castle and announced their arrival to the gatekeeper. Benny could hardly wait to see the amazed expression on Isabella's face. Her wonderful letter, expressing such glad acceptance of his marriage proposal, had filled him with joy and desire. He couldn't wait to see her. So, he had concocted a plan to surprise her. Leaving his militia encamped a few miles away, he and Jeph had galloped to Isabella's home. Now he was at her door, about to sweep his dearest into his arms.

Ben's face fell when a gray-haired steward, not Isabella, approached from the courtyard. It fell even further when the man explained with great apology that Lady Isabella and her attendant had left two days earlier. All he knew was that they were heading for Bailederi Castle to meet the Prince.

"I didn't think it wise for two young damsels to head out by themselves, but they assured me they would be all right and Lady Isabella could not be dissuaded. She told me her mind was made up. She instructed me to keep the Christmas festivities going for the servants here. And that's what I've been doing," the elderly man added.

The Prince bowed respectfully. He and Jeph re-mounted and headed back down the road.

"Well, my man, I guess this means a slight delay in my plan. Nevertheless, I'm bound to yet surprise Lady Isabella. But Jeph, it does concern me to think of those two women travelling unescorted. Drake's battalions are scattered all over this countryside. I pray they don't meet up with any of them."

"Your Highness, there are two ways to get to Bailederi from here... road and river. That red-haired servant of Lady Isabella's strikes me as strong and brave. I wouldn't put it past her to go by river."

"But she would have had to persuade her mistress, and I judge Isabella to prefer riding to rowing. I tell you what... you take the river route and I'll follow the road. Hopefully, they're already safe at Bailederi but, if not, one of us should find them somewhere along the way. We'll meet up at the Castle in a day or two." As they pulled on the reins to head in opposite directions, Benny called back to his friend,

"Jeph, I must admit, this thing called love leads its captives on some very unexpected paths."

Intent on his mission, Benny stopped only long enough to rest and feed his horse and to inquire in each village and hamlet along the way as to whether anyone had noticed two young women journeying through their midst. No one had. He was concluding that they must have gone by way of the river after all. Ahead lay one more town before Bailederi Castle. If the girls weren't there, perhaps they were already safe at his father's house. He hoped with all his heart that Isabella had not fallen into Drake's cruel hands. But he had a nagging sense that she was in danger.

When an angry-looking knight galloped by, that sense turned to certainty. Benny saw the blur of a dragon. One of Drake's men!

"The scoundrel himself is surely close by," Benny concluded.

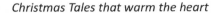
He removed a commoner's cloak from his saddlebag, tying it around him to hide the royal emblem on his tunic. Reaching the crest of the hill, his worst concerns were confirmed. Just below him lay the village and, in the wide plain beyond, was a vast sea of soldiers... Drake's soldiers... encamped only a day's ride from Bailederi.

His father would undoubtedly come under attack any day. The future of the kingdom was at stake. And *somewhere* in all this mess was Isabella.

Benny led his horse as nonchalantly as he could, into the town square. Peasants and merchants, along with groups of Drake's soldiers, filled the narrow streets. Benny was grateful for all the activity. He moved inconspicuously among the crowd and soon spied the building he sought. Tying the reins of his horse to a nearby post, he ducked into the little chapel. Kneeling in prayer at the altar was a young monk. Benny approached and laid his hand on the priest's shoulder. The prince pulled back his cloak to reveal his royal ensign.

"Oh, Your Highness!" the startled cleric jumped to his feet.

"Quiet, my brother. Tell me, can you ride?"

"Yes, Your Highness. I can ride like the wind."

"Do you think you could get to Bailederi Castle without taking the main road?"

"Yes… I know the trails through these woods like I know the Scriptures."

"Well, then I hope you're quite a Bible scholar," Benny chuckled. "And do you have a quill and parchment for me to write a letter?"

"Yes, Your Highness."

He led Benny to a small desk in the back of the room. The prince scribbled his message, pressed his ring below his signature, folded the paper and handed it to the youth.

"Take my horse and ride like Satan himself is chasing you and deliver this message to the King."

"I will, Your Highness. But please be careful. That horrid Drake has overrun our town and talk is that he will soon besiege Bailederi. The townspeople are terrified and feel helpless to stand against him."

"Do you know if Drake is keeping any prisoners?"

"I've heard he's been holding some for days in a shack on the east side of the village."

"A hundred thanks to you, servant of God. You will be richly rewarded for your service. Now be on your way and may the Almighty accompany you."

"He always does, Your Highness." The youthful curate bowed, then hurried out the door.

Benny walked back to the nave of the chapel. On a small table in front of the altar was a simple nativity scene. Beside it stood a crudely-carved wooden cross. Benny gently touched the Christ Child. Then, with both hands, he wrapped his fingers around the cross and drew it close to his heart. Reverently, he knelt at the altar and Prince Benedictus surrendered the coming hours to God. Resolutely, he rose, placed the cross back beside the manger, and headed out to pay whatever price was necessary to rescue a most-precious prisoner.

In the twilight of Epiphany's Eve, two weary pilgrims emerged from the forest. They were worn and battered in body, but strong in spirit. Just ahead loomed their destination, glowing in the golden light of winter's setting sun. As they trudged up to the imposing stone fortress, the gates suddenly swung open, and striding toward them was a most majestic figure. He held out his arms and welcomed them into his embrace. His son and his beloved were home... safe at last.

Hours later, now washed, fed, and warmed, the couple sat with the King in his chamber and implored him to tell them what had transpired over the last few days. They knew, of course, their part of the saga. After the Prince managed to overpower her guards and free Isabella from her shackles in the shed on the outskirts of the village, the two had fled on foot into the forest. Isabella, weak from days with no food, had to lean heavily on Benny who himself sported several nasty gashes gained in his encounter with her captors. They travelled far from the enemy-ridden plain below the village. But as they made their circuitous journey, evidently a lot was happening elsewhere.

"Having been warned of Drake's approach," the Monarch began, "I sent messengers throughout the kingdom. Loyal subjects from far and wide, along with our own forces, rallied and surrounded Drake and his men. The battle was intense, but brief and decisive. We'll not be needing to deal with that rogue knight ever again."

"But how did you gather so many fighters?" Benny asked.

"Oh, when it comes to my son and his lovely bride, I would call all of heaven and earth, if necessary, to bring them safely home."

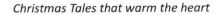
"But how did you rally them so quickly?" Benny persisted. "That monk could only have provided a day or less of warning."

"No, the monk reached us almost a week before the battle began. That didn't give us much time, but thankfully it was sufficient to summon extra forces."

"That's impossible," Benny insisted. "I met him in the village chapel only three days ago. I told him to fly, but he certainly couldn't have arrived more than a day before the battle."

"Oh, *that* monk!" the King chuckled. "You're right. He arrived just shortly before the fighting began. It was the *other* monk that sounded the alarm in time for us to prepare."

As if on cue, the chamber door swung open and an elderly cleric with a broad grin and twinkling eyes stood before them.

"That's him," the King announced. "I think you know him well, Son."

"Friar Jon!" Benny rose and embraced the old gentleman. "I should have known!"

Now it was Isabella on her feet.

"Friar Jon?" she exclaimed. "I feel like I already know you. I've heard all about you. Marelee..." her voice broke.

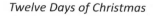
"Marelee, my handmaiden, quoted you always. She said you were her best friend. But sadly, Marelee's dead."

Isabella buried her head on Benny's shoulder.

"Now, now… no need to cry, m'Lady. Friar Jon says what we thinks is the end is often just the beginning."

Isabella's head jerked up at the sound of a wonder-fully-familiar voice.

"Marelee!" she shouted and, in a flash, the two young women were hugging and laughing with delight. "I thought you had perished!" Isabella cried.

"Truly me thought so too, when that awful Drake slugged me. The blow stunned me, but m'life t'weren't over yet. I lay there a'wondering what t'do and then I remembered Friar Jon always said, 'When thy enemy rushes in the front door, look for a back window!' So that's what I decided to do. When they dragged thee out and shut the door, I dove through that back window as the flames licked me heels. Then I rolled like a roly-poly hedgehog into the woods. When I heard the horses ride off, me headed for our boat. And who should be there waiting for me but…"

"Friar Jon!" Isabella guessed.

"That's right and we rowed like crazy until that old dingy sprung a leak and we started to sink. Me near died a second time. I thought Friar Jon would get

us t'shore, but he said walkin' on water was not his special'ty... only Jesus had mastered that. If it hadn't been for another miracle rescuer, we'd both have drowned in the river."

"What do you mean?" Isabella implored. "Who rescued you?"

"I admit that was me," a male voice boomed from the hallway. A tall, handsome young knight joined the group.

"Jeph!" Benny was by his side, bear-hugging his assistant and slapping him on the back.

"Yes, Jeph pulled alongside us in a much sturdier craft and hauled us both safely aboard. It was quite a feat, considering my size," Friar Jon chuckled. "With three sets of strong arms rowing hard, we made it to Bailederi in short order and alerted His Majesty that Drake was nearby and plotting attack. The King sounded the alarm and the rest of the story you know."

Prince Benedictus sighed and surveyed the happy group.

"You know, tomorrow ends the twelve days of Christmas. We will commemorate the coming of the wise men to Jesus... our King of love... all those years ago. It seems so fitting that our own perilous Christmas journeys have ended in such joy. I believe Epiphany would be perfect if it were to include a celebration... a celebra-

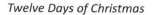

tion of love. Friar Jon, would you be willing to perform a wedding tomorrow? Isabella and I talked this over on our journey back home. We have waited long enough!" Benny looked at his bride expectantly.

"What do you say, my darling? You did bring your dancing shoes in that old sack, didn't you?"

In answer, Isabella squealed with delight and threw her arms around Benny.

Friar Jon stroked his chin.

"Well now, that might be difficult since I have a prior commitment on the morrow right here at the castle."

Benny's face fell.

"Of course, if the other couple would agree, I suppose I could conduct two weddings." Friar Jon cocked his head toward Jeph and Marelee who were now standing tight against each other, arms linked.

They laughed and nodded. Marelee spoke up,

"You see, m'Lady, Sir Jephridous was the childhood chum I told thee about. I thought when he left and became a high n' mighty soldier that he'd never think of me again." She flashed a smile at Jeph who was beaming at her, love shining in his eyes. "I was wrong. But truly, Friar Jon... His Highness and Lady Isabella...

well, they're *royalty*. Jeph and me... we can wait to be married another day."

Isabella hastened to the servant couple and clasped their hands in hers.

"You two risked your lives for Benny and me. You are *not* servants. You are *friends!* I think a double wedding will be so much better than my very best dream!"

"However, Friar Jon," Isabella spun to face the old monk. "I know they're just letters on a page, but do you think on their marriage certificate you could spell my friend's name... M-E-R-R-I-L-Y?!"

And so that Christmas ended just as the very first Christmas had... with a beginning. For a King, a Prince and his bride, their friends, and a funny little old cleric who managed to show up precisely when needed, there was so much more yet to come.

With great wisdom and much love, they would rule their precious kingdom together, and they would all live very, very merrily forevermore!

Made in the USA
Monee, IL
03 November 2020